PROPHET OF THE GODSEED

Part 1 of Deep Time

By

David Van Dyke Stewart

©2016 David Van Dyke Stewart. All rights reserved. This work may not be reprinted, in whole or in part, for profit or not, without prior express written permission of the author. Elements from this story were originally published in 2014-2016 on dvspress.com in a different format. Based on *Deep Time,* created by David V. Stewart and Matthew J. Wellman.

"Burdens of the Patriarch" ©2015 Matthew J. Wellman. All rights reserved.

This is a work of fiction. All characters and events portrayed herein are fictitious; historical persons are used fictitiously and this work should not constitute a work of history or scholarship.

Cover Design by David V. Stewart with photography by Galyna Andrushko, Anelina, and NASA.

For Matty, who created with me,

For Houkje, who created on my behalf,

And

For Gene, who inspired me to think of great journeys.

Contents

Chapter 1 - Karakûm.. 1

Chapter 2 - Greywing 15

Memory – Simple Tasks... 35

Chapter 3 - Macbeth.. 39

Memory - Twins Across Two Times.................... 57

Chapter 4 – The Gate 67

Chapter 5 – Fires of the Past................................. 87

Bread Upon the Water 107

Chapter 6 – Unity and Separation 129

Chapter 7 – Fire Ark 143

Drawn from the Water... 163

Chapter 8 – The Citadel..................................... 177

Chapter 9 – Prophet.. 191

Epilogue – Black Coffee 207

Burdens of the Patriarch...................................... 213

About the Author.. 225

Prophet of the Godseed

CHAPTER 1
Karakûm

T HE DESERT. That is where prophets are made.
Across the vast wastes of time, when each year past is but a grain of sand and each world gained or lost is but a chapter of a book, the desert remains as it always has been. The dry, endless waves of sand have always meant something to men of faith. Hot, desolate, waterless... only a man of God can survive, and only with the blessing of God, or so it seems.

Karakûm. The Place of Burning. *Drogathalum.* The Sea of Sand. It marched all the way from the mountains of drought, Staltutum, to the steaming sea, or Drog'ta. The sea was the only sure place to find water for a thousand leagues, and it was boiling in the endless sun, sending storms raging across the savanna to the west and toward the Shadowlands, the night side of Terranostra. Still, in a land with as few goals as features, it was perhaps the only workable quest, as unfeasible as it seemed. There would be people there, farming and living off the grace of the savanna, and men manning the massive power plants for the larger cities in the habitable zone. If only there was a way to get there without walking.

"Oh, Padalmo, what were you thinking?" the young man said to himself. "You're no more a prophet than a karatoid. You are probably as likely to sprout wings and fly out of here as you are to encounter God." He sat underneath an overhanging rock which made for him a small cave, watching the piles of sand shift outside in the endless desert. The wind was howling, but it was also burning hot.

He had been left without a communicator, a computer, or any means of telling the time. He wondered how long he would have to wait for the winds to subside, when he could begin walking again. He prayed for Clouds to come and mute and blur the sun for a time, lessening its oppression enough for Padalmo to brave the sands. Of course, he could still sweat out all the water they had given him between this rock and the next shelter he came across, even with cloud cover. He looked at the shadows. They were still very sharp.

Padalmo wondered if the people on the dark side did the same thing to their high houses each generation, sending volunteers to go in search of God, wandering their endless snow in eternal dark beneath white stars, just as the faithful wandered the endless sand beneath in everlasting day and blue-white sky. He supposed the Darksiders had a god, whatever he was. Padalmo knew, however foolish he might be in his own search, that the Darksiders didn't really believe in the true God. Any god they believed in would have to be a false god; heedless were they of the words of the Seeders.

PROPHET OF THE GODSEED

The Seeders warned us of the dangers of exceeding our technological limits. This one truth we have held. I may not be their prophet, but when they return, they will be pleased that we have halted the progress of the Darksiders.

Padalmo snickered to himself. "Do I really believe that? The Seeders are never returning. God will not be with them." He leaned up against one of the sides of the little half-cave. His eyes felt dry despite his moisture-retaining suit. "If I'm going to die out here, I might as well not die sleepy." He closed his eyes behind dark goggles.

He imagined he was talking to his father, Highlord of Tala'Drog'chu, arrayed in his overlapping cloth mantle and his many war medals. He wore the same sour face as always; he was ever disappointed in his twelfth son, who had refused the call to arms for the latest war. At twenty-two Padalmo was a man without prestige and with no wives to call his own.

"You always look so disappointed in me, father."

"That's because you *are* a disappointment to me," the image said. *No, he wouldn't just say that. For all his faults, my father is at least kind to his children.* "I just want you achieve greatness, and carry on the family name."

"War is death, father. How can you not see that?"

His father crossed his arms. "The holy wars are what separate the grain from the chaff. They are death only for the unworthy. That is why our line is strongest, even among the highlords. Only those who are worthy come back to claim our fortune. I wish you would make the attempt."

"I'm making a different attempt."

"You never struck me as the faithful type, son. I figured that was why you avoided the army. You are afraid of death." Padalmo imagined his father's surprised face when he told him that he was attempting the trial of the prophet, and found he could not place it the image he now envisioned.

"I'm not afraid of death, as you can see," Padalmo said.

"Hmph. I know better. You have something in mind."

"I did." Padalmo hung his head. Travole, his childhood friend, a commoner with a single wife, was supposed to come out and retrieve him. He had no way of telling time in the endless sun, but he knew that his friend was long overdue. Padalmo retrieved the beacon from his pocket. Its light glowed softly.

"Not content to try yourself in fire, and earn your appropriate prestige," the image of the Highlord went on, despite Padalmo wishing it to be silent, "You had to try to be the *prophet*. You always want to be greater than your brothers, but you never apply yourself like them! You want to be the prophet because of what it offers you!"

"Quiet!"

"You want to live like me, but you want don't want the effort of office. You want more wives than me, and none widows! You want a citadel instead of a high house!"

That's not him, that's me. Padalmo sighed and shut his eyes. *I'll get some sleep, then I'll see how the sun is.*

*

Padalmo dreamt uneasily. He saw the transport that had left him in the desert, in randomly determined location according to tradition and the teachings of the Seeders, as it lifted off the ground. He saw the eyes of the pilot, filled with pity at a man who was a fool, sure to die soon. The image repeated several times, and the pilot's face, a stranger's face, was replaced with the familiar visage of Travole. He held the same sorry look.

"I knew you'd come!" Padalmo shouted. His friend, however, did not acknowledge him, but instead lifted away and flew south to the dark mountains.

Eventually the dream shifted to other, more mundane things. He was eating dinner at his father's great table on the palace veranda. The light curtains stirred with the north wind, and two of his father's wives stared at him, one frowning and one hiding a smile. He was in a room in his brother's apartments, playing a board game. He was wandering the halls of the harem, talking to one of his sisters. Travole's face appeared on a balcony overlooking the sea. A storm was coming, and they laughed and smoked, and drank, with Travole's wife, who looked as she did when they were children.

*

Padalmo woke to darkness. It was not the darkness of drapes drawn on the sunward side of a house during a sleep period, which was deep and overwhelming, but rather a soft, rippling diffusion of light. He could see the sand outside the rock overhang, sitting still in piles and dunes where it once was shifting. The shadow of the rock itself blended with the color of grey sand outside.

A storm, Padalmo thought. *There's not supposed to be storms over this part of the desert for another quarter year.* He crept out and looked at the sky. Large billows of low clouds, ranging from slight grey to near black, raced overhead, stretching over the plains of rock and sand as far as Padalmo could see in either direction. The wind on the planet's surface was still calm, a relief from the burning hot gales that ever shifted the sands of Karakûm. Storm winds would come later. How long had he slept, to miss the calm front of a storm, so far from the sea of Drog'ta?

"By the grace of the Seeders, what a relief," Padalmo said. He removed the scarf and goggles that had protected his face against the biting bits of silica that had been swirling painfully about him before. A short, black beard stood out below a pronounced nose. Blue eyes blazed, surrounded by skin darkened to a deep, chocolate brown. He breathed deeply, glad to feel fresh air once again. No air smelled as good as the front of a storm, especially in the habitable zone, with its constant reek of industry and human life. He understood now how pure the air must feel in the safe areas around the burning sea.

This is God's breath, he thought, and smiled. Perhaps he could find faith on this journey after all. He removed from a pocket his compass, an ancient tool but invaluable if you took the teachings of the Seeders to heart and chose not to rely too heavily on technology.

He watched the red needle fly about and point off to his left. In the habitable zone, you would need the sun's constant position to figure out where the weak north and strong south poles were of Terranostra, and therefore plot your direction. On the sun side such efforts became unnecessary, as the compass would always point true south.

Padalmo figured his positioning, then plotted a course that would take him relatively to the north-east, to the steaming sea. He took a look back at the small rock group that had been his home for... how long was it? He could not reckon. The formation felt significant to him, partly because of the revelations it had given him through the remembrance of his father, and partly because he knew he would never see it again.

"Farewell, shelter of peace. May you give to the next prophet what you have given to me." He said a silent prayer to God and set off.

Part of him worried about the unexpected storm. Rarely did such storms drop much moisture sunward of the Staltutum Mountains, but if this one did, which seemed likely given how dark the clouds were, it would turn Drogothalum into Drogothured, a sea of quick sand. *Water is life. A flood is death. How delicate we truly are.*

"God will provide me shelter, if it comes to that," Padalmo said to himself. "I go with God's will now."

He walked quickly beneath the leaden sky, the sand moving harshly under his wide-soled boots. His lips parted his dark beard into a smile.

*

The rain came. It proved to be a blessing, not a curse. Rather than the torrential downpour Padalmo was expecting, having seen only the storms in the habitable zone and upon the Mountains of drought. This rain was sparse, unloading heavy drops of water for a few minutes at a time, then ceasing. The water cooled Padalmo's face, and during a few showers he was able to catch some drops in his water collector, essentially a funnel that filled his expandable bladders. He might have enough moisture to complete the journey on his own terms, an encouraging thought after Travole's failure to retrieve him. The rain also provided an unexpected benefit with the sand, which would soak up the water and then quickly dry, leaving a crust that made walking on the dunes between rock formations much easier.

How long would it take him to reach the Steaming Sea? He did not know, for he had no better an understanding of the passage of time under the storm than he did under the changeless, ever-shining sun. He felt confident he would get there, alive and in one piece. He had drank his fill while keeping his water bladders full, and had even stopped to urinate a few times on the walk.

"It's funny how good it feels to make water when you simply haven't been able to for a long time," he said to nobody. "Even better than holding it, if you ask me."

He could see the end of the storm now, as a bright shining stripe of white sand on the sunward horizon. It was growing, but Padalmo was sure he would come across shelter before it arrived to bake him once more.

*

No shelter appeared for Padalmo. The storm had flown away, nightward toward the Barrier Mountains and the jungles on their steppes, leaving the young man turned prophet in the blazing, undimming sun once again. It hovered off to his right, lower in the sky than where he had been, but not yet low enough to be less than deadly. Beneath his robes, scarf, goggles, and moisture suit, he sweated profusely. He longed to remove them all, but the sand, which swirled again with the loss of the storm, would have carved his flesh to a bloody pulp. His bladders were growing lighter as well, and he felt parched.

"This is just another test," Padalmo said, heaving his boots through the loose sand. "Salvation comes always at the edge of death. God needs a prophet who trusts, and is unafraid of death." He said it aloud, hoping he would believe it, but the old doubts were returning. Self-hatred and fear presented themselves again, marking his inner self as an unworthy messenger for the almighty.

The sand stretched on ahead of him, unchanging. No clouds sprang up to give him cover and blessed life. Drog'ta was invisible. Drogathalum was ever-present, destroying him.

I have no choice but to believe in the salvation ahead. For if not for that, I will die anyway. Either I am the prophet or not.

Death, at long last.

Padalmo was crawling now. His legs had grown too tired and weak to continue shoveling through the sand. He got better traction crawling, though the infinitely small particles of silica slipped through his fingers like they were water.

"I am a child again," he said aloud. His voice croaked. "You must become like a child to enter the kingdom of God. So be it, either I enter now, crawling like a baby, or I become its prophet."

His mind was flooded with vivid memories of his home, the high house of Tala'Drog'Chu, the mansion of Imalmo, his father. Joy for Padalmo existed in the casual existence of growing up in the harem, away from the busy streets of Pana'Chu, the bay city his family had ruled for innumerable generations. He studied texts alongside his brothers, all of whom had eventually left for the war against the infidels, one-by-one, leaving Padalmo behind. He teased his sisters, who one-by-one were married off to other high houses, strengthening the alliance of the Faithful, or given as reward to a loyal servant of the city-state.

It was a simple, but lush experience. He never went hungry. Never had to go without, or have unfulfilled desire. He had never wanted more, but everyone, Imalmo in particular, had demanded that he want more. Pursue more. That meant war and death, just to get back what he had lived with his whole life. It was bitter.

He missed them all now, even his father, seeing his death before him, but he missed most Fala. Fala, who had made him a man while he still lived as a boy in the harem. Fala, who had taught him the ways of women as much as the ways of his own body. Sweet Fala, with blooms in her tawny hair. He thought of her body, slick under his. He felt her breasts, her legs wrapped around his hips, and her arms around his neck. She had taken from him when he could not understand as a boy. As a man, he had grown to need what she took. He was suddenly wracked with guilt about his relationship with her. Fala, forbidden fruit.

He longed for her the most. He missed her council. She had helped him avoid the war. She had not wanted him to make the prophet's journey, but had understood why he needed to. Did he love her, after all?

"I do love you, Fala. I love you. Forgive me."

*

Padalmo was back in the bay, under the twisting foliage, blocking the sun, which was low in the sky. A cool breeze dried his sweaty face. Fala was there, wearing a long, silken gown whose revelation of the curves of her body would be acceptable only in the seclusion of a harem. Her green eyes stared at him. She was not smiling. Padalmo wanted her to smile. She poured a glass of some liquid, which was red. She handed it to him. He drank. It was sweet.

"I'm sorry."

Fala was silent as she set her drink down and began untying his robes.

"I'm the prophet now. I could take you for myself, if I wanted."

Fala looked up at him. Her green eyes blazed. She reached up to her shoulders and pulled the straps of her gown. The garment fell down, sticking on her hips and exposing her breasts. Padalmo felt his hands reaching for her hips, and pulling the gown the rest of the way off.

They were suddenly making love, fervently. She was silent, staring at him. His ears were filled with the sound of rushing water beside them. He realized the shore of the bay was rising. The table was tipped over, and his body was struck with cold, harsh water. They were carried up in the deluge. Padalmo reached out for Fala, but she had already been born away from him. He plunged under the water, and saw the ruin of the palace.

*

The dream vanished, and Padalmo opened his eyes. He was still in the desert. His face covering had fallen away, and he could feel sand sticking to his lips. His hat lay under his head, failing to shield him from the harsh sun. He tried to cry out, but could not. His throat and lungs were dry, dying.

Why couldn't I die in the dream? he thought. His mind searched out again for the vision, and he realized that he was cold. The wind was blowing harshly, enough to pull away what moisture remained in his robes and moisture suit, cooling him quickly. Flying sand obscured his vision.

The wind intensified, gusts blowing sand into Padalmo's mouth. He squeezed it shut and tried to move.

He craned his neck to see that his body was partially buried in sand.

Nobody will ever find me. The wind became even stronger, and out of the blinding blizzard of silica flecks, Padalmo saw something he had never seen before.

A grey object appeared, hovering some fifty feet off the ground.

A transport? Perhaps Travole has come for me at last. It is too much to dream.

As it neared, Padalmo could make out what looked like exhaust ports, glowing a bright blue. The roar of its engines overpowered the wind. It neared and flew lower, passing over him and moving out of his vision. He could feel vibrations through the sand.

After a few minutes he felt hands groping him. Sand was pouring off of his body, but even relieved of the weight, he found he could not move his appendages. He had truly become like a baby, unable to lift himself or even crawl. He was being carried by his shoulders and feet. He looked up at the sky, a pale and stark vanilla-blue.

A face filled his vision. A bald man, with a smooth brown face. He was smiling slightly. He was speaking, but the words were incomprehensible. It reminded him of the high-speech, which he had learned from birth in recitation of the holy texts. The old tongue, but everything was being pronounced incorrectly. He heard another voice speaking in the same manner.

Padalmo drifted away.

CHAPTER 2
Greywing

PADALMO DREAMT nothing more. Fala did not come to comfort him. He awoke to the sounds of machinery, humming quietly and clicking away in uncertain rhythms, and was aware of a soft repeating tone. He forced his eyes open. The ceiling was a cool white interrupted by grey lines intersecting one another in squares. He tried moving his head and found he could move slightly to either side, though it hurt gravely to do so. He could see that he was on some sort of bed, only it was raised off the ground a few feet. There were similar, empty ones off to each side. Tubes and wires hung down in his view.

He had heard the Darksiders slept in beds high off the ground. Strange. Perhaps it was they who had saved him. Or was he captured? Strange mercies, to be saved by the enemy. Perhaps he was saved for a purpose. Perhaps they knew of his father, and would question him.

The seeders, he thought, as memories of his rescue returned to him. The strange bald man, speaking what he knew was the ancient tongue of the holy texts, only strange and foul. Perhaps the seeders had returned, as stated in the prophesies. *I would be the prophet, then. The true prophet, not the figure-head they parade around Pana'Chu who just says the same old things.* A pain assaulted Padalmo behind his eyes. *No, that cannot be it. I never had the true faith.*

He closed his eyes again quickly as he heard voices. It was a man and a woman. They were speaking the same strange words the bald man used during the rescue, and Padalmo was assured of its origin. It was the holy language. It was the church that had spoken it wrong. Only a few words could he understand, while the others were reminiscent of the old tongue. The voices neared.

"Are you awake?" the male voice said. Padalmo was surprised to understand him, although he seemed to have an accent like a Darksider, or one of the enemy factions in the south end of the inhabitable zone. He had heard so many accents on the state updates that flashed on the vid screens daily he had a hard time really placing it, except that he knew it was not from Pana'Chu.

Padalmo opened his eyes and strained to speak. "Where-" His larynx stung as if it were pierced with needles.

"You're onboard Greywing, one of the orbiting autonomous sections of Icarus," the man said. It was indeed the same man who had picked him up out of the sand. He was smiling. Padalmo noticed small metal ornaments on the man's temples and behind one of his ears.

The woman said something he didn't understand. Padalmo turned his head to see her. She was older, with long grey hair and a stern face. Her skin was incredibly pale, but her eyes were blue like the people of bay. The bald man spoke back to her with a pliant tone. She crossed her arms as if she were a superior to him. Strange. A woman telling a man what to do.

"Sorry about that, I've been informed that you don't really know anything I'm talking about. My name is Moses," the bald man said. "We've done our best to clean the silica dust out of your lungs and repair the tissue damage you suffered, but things may hurt for a while."

"I am Padalmo." Pain. Not as bad as the first attempt.

The woman said something to the man again. He nodded to her.

"Sorry. I am pleased to meet you, Padalmo." The man touched one of the metal things on his head. "May God always show you the path to truth." It was a common greeting at the temple.

Who is this man? Padalmo swallowed needles.

"You should get some sleep. We'll try to do more tissue repairs later, and then we can have a-" Moses looked at the woman. She was speaking harshly at him. "This is Captain Claribel. Sorry I didn't introduce you."

The old woman reached forward and grabbed Padalmo's hand, then shook it up and down.

What is this about? Padalmo thought. The woman said something else to Moses. Moses looked back at him.

"We'll talk more when you feel better," he said. "The captain will give you something to ease your pain and help you sleep.

Padalmo nodded, then closed his eyes and relaxed his head. The sound of machinery filled his ears as footsteps retreated, echoing.

*

"I thought it would prove advantageous to retrieve someone who clearly would not be missed from the major populated areas, at least for a while. A man dead to this world," Claribel said. She stood with her feet shoulder-width apart, her hands relaxed behind her back. Moses thought she looked very strong as she stared at the com screen displaying the clan chieftain. Malcom Macbeth looked as calm and in control as ever, but Moses was learning to recognize the hints of emotion in people's body language. The clan leader was frowning.

"We also saved a life," Moses said, cutting in, hoping to deflect some of the chieftain's anger. "The sun-locked side of the planet is most inhospitable." He immediately regretted opening his mouth, unsure of why he rushed to defend the captain, especially out of turn.

"I wasn't addressing you, Moses," Malcolm said calmly.

"Sorry, sir." Moses looked down.

"Keep it in mind," the Clan leader said, smiling slightly. "We have rank order for good reasons. But you are right, you did save a life. Why do you think that is a defense?"

"Because you value life," Moses said. "Or I wouldn't be here."

"Be that as it may, Moses," Malcolm said, "we cannot save every life along the way. There are billions and billions of humans spread across the galaxy, and we could not save them, even if it were our mission, which it is not."

"Sir, is this conversation relevant?" Claribel said, glancing over to Moses. "We have a limited time table, or so I thought."

"Learning is always relevant, captain," Malcolm said. "Besides, your man is unconscious, and Tully and I are finding the quantum gate to be a bit bigger task than we had originally anticipated."

"Is that so?" Claribel said, raising an eyebrow. "Rare for Tully to admit she's in over her head."

"I'm not in over my head!" A high-pitched voiced piped from the background of the com screen. A young woman appeared in the background, seated in a metal chair. She had a mane of red hair and pale, freckled skin. "You want to try your hand at decrypting this ancient pile of junk?"

Malcom frowned and looked to the side. "I designed this pile of junk, you know. I'd say it's held up quite well considering how long it's been derelict. And you're out of turn." He looked back at the com screen. "Keep me posted on the planetsider."

"Sir, there's something else," Claribel said. "It's Moses. It seems some of his implants – the ones we were afraid to remove when we picked him up – have reactivated."

"Interesting," Malcolm said. He looked past Claribel to Moses.

"They are interfacing with networks planet-side," she went on. "Using our signal amplifiers, he's been able to access a host of servers on part of the planet's internet. Purely a user-oriented experience, for right now."

"So you think that they are in danger of collectivizing," Malcolm said.

"It's a possibility," Claribel said. "Of course, only part of the planet seems to be using implant technology, but it would explain the deactivated quantum gate. Maybe this planet's trade partners saw what was coming and pulled the plug before the planet could reach singularity."

"Not quite!" Tully piped in. Moses craned his head around Claribel to see her move off the com screen again. "The gate was closed on this side!"

"You're out of turn again, Tully," Malcom said, much more cross than when he had spoken to Moses.

"Sorry sir," Tully said quietly.

PROPHET OF THE GODSEED

"She reminds me of myself," Claribel said, smiling. "Go easy on her."

Malcolm nodded. "Aye. She does remind me of you."

Is that a good or a bad thing? Moses thought to himself. He hadn't gotten to talk to Tully much lately, but she was one of the first people to warm up to him. *Maybe this is what it means to miss somebody. I'll talk to Anders about it.*

Malcolm continued. "I was made aware of the de-activation back on Rondella Duo by our descendants there, but they had no knowledge of how the gate was closed. I suspected it could have been one of the other clans, though nobody would openly break the peace. We can rest that fear for now, but there are new mysteries we are finding up here."

"How long has the gate been closed?" Claribel said.

"We're working on figuring that out," Malcolm said. "Re-activating it is a slow process, and we're having to pipe in auxiliary power from the ship. My guess is, taking in the status of the planet below, it's been a few centuries, if not millennia."

"Long time," Claribel said.

"Only to some," Malcom said. "Keep me posted, captain. I'll let you know what Tully and I find out. Macbeth out."

Claribel nodded as the vid screen went dark.

*

Padalmo grimaced as he swallowed another spoonful of the strange, semi-solid grey substance. He would not have known it was food had he not seen the bald man slurp down half a bowl himself. *Moses. I like that name. It has a godly quality to it.* He looked at the bald man, sitting in a chair beside Padalmo's bed in the long room that made what Padalmo assumed to be part of a hospital. Now conscious, he could take in more clearly the image of the man beside him, who was tall and lean. He wore a simple set of green-hued pants and a loose fitting grey jacket over a similarly grey shirt. The bits of metal on his head seemed to be growing right out of the skin. They looked electronic to Padalmo's eyes, but he could not be certain. It unsettled him, as he recalled reports of the Darksiders using implant technology in violation of the Seeders' directives.

"Is the food not to your liking?" Moses said, with his strange, other-worldly accent.

Paldamo smiled and looked back at Moses. He looked oddly child-like as he stared back at Padalmo, with his dark and lineless face, and the dark eyes which poured over him without looking away. Did he have different manners, or did he have no manners?

"It's better than nothing," Padalmo said, and forced down another spoonful.

"Of course it is," Moses said. He cocked his head away for a moment. "Were you being facetious?"

"I was being truthful," Padalmo said. "But the way I said it could have been an insult. I apologize."

Moses nodded. "Better than nothing, but not necessarily good. I see. You don't like it then?"

"No, I find it rather bad," Padalmo said. "But that does not mean I am not grateful. Frankly, I don't know the last time I ate. They say hunger is the finest seasoning, but I am finding that truism a bit lacking." He stared at the grey mush in his bowl.

Moses stared at him a moment, unblinking. "I understand. Yes. When we are hungry, we are much more willing to accept substandard food because of the need for nutrition."

Padalmo laughed. "You don't have to explain it to me."

"The chieftain says it is good to explain things to myself." Moses shook his head. "Sorry, I forgot you don't know who I'm talking about. Also," he looked down at the food. "I realize that I have made a bad assumption. I have fed you the food that I myself prefer, without taking into account that you might have different tastes than me. I apologize. If you are feeling up to it, I can take you down to the wing's food facilities. There should be better accommodation there."

Moses stood and motioned for Padalmo to get up. Padalmo put the bowl down on a nearby table and swung his legs out over the bed. He felt his bare toes dangle a bit, then pushed himself out of the bed. His legs ached as he put weight on them, but he felt strong. He realized he was clothed only in a simple white undergarment.

Moses looked at him. "We'll need to get you some clothes. I think I have some spare scrubs around here somewhere. I'll be right back." The bald man hurried to the end of the elongated room. Padalmo flinched as part of the wall opened up, and Moses stepped through. He returned with a pile of clothes in a dull grey and placed them on the bed. "I'll give you some privacy. I'll be right outside the door." Padalmo nodded. Moses walked back to the edge of the room. The door opened up and he disappeared behind it.

Padalmo quickly put on the clothes, which consisted of a loose fitting pair of pants and long-sleeved shirt. Both were made of a soft material that felt like fibrilin. The shoes had no laces or other means of securing them to the feet that Padalmo could see, but after some effort he managed to shove them on. He took a deep breath and looked around the room. He saw four beds, and some consoles. A rolling table stood nearby the section of wall that should be the door. A few pieces of metal and a plastic bag sat idly on it.

Am I in the house of the gods? He was doubtful. Though there were definitely strange things here, Moses, for all his eccentricities, was still human. That much was sure. Padalmo took a deep breath and shuffled toward the end of the room. He was surprised when, from no input of his own, the door opened for him. He found Moses waiting on the other side.

"Ah, good," Moses said, looking him up and down. "Follow me." Padalmo nodded and followed Moses through another set of doors which looked more to their purpose than the sliding wall in the room full of beds.

PROPHET OF THE GODSEED

They entered a long hallway, and through glass on either side Padalmo could see machines in a bone white, and screens for what looked like computer terminals.

"Where are we?" Padalmo said, almost off-hand.

"We are in the medical department of grey wing," Moses said, turning around and smiling at Padalmo. "This is my current station. These are some of the department's medical machines." He pointed through the glass at a large cylindrical object with an opening at one end. "That is our advanced tissue regenerator. Captain Claribel and I used it to repair your damaged lungs."

"So, you're a doctor?"

"No, I have no specialty yet. The chieftain thought it would be a good, low-pressure assignment for me. We almost never need medical facilities, except for the health maintenance of the clan members, and most of them are in great shape." Moses smiled. "You are actually my first emergency patient."

Padalmo cocked his head. "The chieftain? The clan?"

Moses shook his head again. "I'm sorry. I'm forgetting about you again. I'm not very good at explaining things to others." He gestured for Padalmo to follow him. They went out another set of doors and into another hallway, this one narrow and windowless.

"Where are we?"

"We're in between departments."

"No, I mean, where is *all* of this?" Padalmo stopped in his tracks and looked around at the cramped hallway. "Are we in the dark zone? Is this facility near the steaming sea? Do you work for one of the power consortiums? Are you a Darksider? Are you with one of the side-factions of the Drog'Chu alliance? Where is Travole, if he had anything to do with this?"

Moses paused. "What is the last thing you remember?"

"You and a grey-haired woman talking to me. I was in bed."

"Before that?"

"My home – no, the desert. I was in the desert, and then a transport arrived."

"So you do not remember the journey up here," Moses said. He scratched his chin. "I can see why you're confused. We are not part of any faction, either allied with or in opposition to anyone. We are currently onboard a spacecraft orbiting the planet you call Terranostra."

Padalmo frowned and stared at the strange, bald man. *Orbiting Terranostra...*

"That means that our spacecraft is moving around the planet," Moses said. He put out his fist and moved his other index finger around it in a circle.

"Yes, I know what orbiting means," Padalmo said. "We have satellites..." He shook his head. "How do I know you aren't lying? All I see is the inside of a metal box."

PROPHET OF THE GODSEED

Moses puzzled at this, scrunching his brow. He looked off for a low moment, as if in thought, then looked back, wide-eyed. "If we were part of some faction of your society, why would I let you walk around? Wouldn't have you locked up in like a prisoner?" Moses said. He smirked and walked toward the end of the hall.

"I suppose," Padalmo said, following behind uneasily.

"Then put it out of your mind." The door at the end of the hallway opened and Moses stepped through to a larger meeting of passage-ways.

"And what about the orbiting part?" Padalmo said, rushing to catch up. "Am I just supposed to trust you?"

"No need," Moses said. He stopped at the intersection of two catwalks and leaned against an upright computer terminal. He put his hand over the edge of the rail and pointed down.

Padalmo followed Moses's finger, leaning over the guard-rails that lined the walkway.

Below him was an abyss of circling white light where the floor of the chamber should have been. Dominating the view was a large, round object, mostly dark but edged with a bright, yellow light. He could only see perhaps a quarter of it, but he knew from what he could see it was Terranostra. He stepped back from the edge, vertigo overcoming him, and shook his head.

"Nice view, huh?" Moses said. He had a wide smile watching Padalmo react.

Padalmo collapsed to his knees, breath catching in his throat as his mind rejected his vision. He coughed and sputtered. Moses quickly knelt down beside him.

"Are you alright?" Moses said.

Padalmo took a deep breath in an effort to slow his respiration and speak. "I don't know," he panted.

"It's a lot to take in, eh?" Moses said. "I felt that way the first time I was here. I should have anticipated it. I'll fetch you a drug for your anxiety."

"No drugs," Padalmo said. He reached out and gripped Moses's arm as he tried to stand. Moses sat back down and Padalmo patted him on the shoulder. "I'll be fine. No drugs."

Moses nodded and gazed at him silently. After a time, Padalmo turned himself and looked through the rail at the planet below.

"We're over the dark side," Padalmo said.

"Yes, we are," Moses said. "Your sun was putting out a lot of EM interference. This side gives us some shelter from that, but also has let us probe the planetary net a little bit. In fact the only way I've learned how to talk to you is from querying your internet."

"Not *our* internet," Padalmo said. He looked at Moses with a sudden realization. "That's why you talk like a heretic. You learned to speak by accessing their internet."

"You don't have a single internet?" Moses said.

"No, we've cut ours off from the heretics on the south pole, and in the shadowlands. Those networks are forbidden."

"Forbidden by whom?"

Padalmo looked down at his hands. "By the holy texts."

"Your religion prohibits you from looking at the internet?"

"*Their* internet, yes."

"Interesting. I'm sure the chieftain will want to know all about it. For now, how about some more food? Or some coffee?"

Padalmo did not have time to respond, as Moses began walking down one of the cat-walks, another door at the end of the hall opening for him.

*

They sat in the middle of Greywing's small mess-hall, a view of the stars visible out a window of transparent aluminum. The place was deserted except for him and the man Claribel had reluctantly agreed to save, for which Moses was thankful. He did not want to try managing social graces while managing his hungry patient.

Moses watched as Padalmo greedily ate down the synthesized dry fruit and imitation meat. He had ended up resorting to showing the planetsider pictures of the food the synthesizer could make. None of the descriptions seemed to make sense to the man, and the planetside network wasn't much help either.

Moses taped into the internet again, feeling what he liked to call his "electronic fingers" probe their way into an array of servers that could relay him back simple linguistic information. For more obscure words in English, the language of the Macbeth clan and all its holdings, he found that he could get accurate translations quite easily with search queries. It was almost natural to him, like being home on Earth, though he could scarcely remember the time he had spent there.

"Is this food *tastier* than the other?" he asked in the Terranostra language. He stowed the meaning of the new word away in his local storage, just in case.

"God, yes," Padalmo said through a full mouth.

"Good for you. I can barely stand most of the food the synthesizer puts out. I find it too strong."

"Too strong?" Padalmo said. He held out a fruit: a date. "This is delicious."

Padalmo took it from his hand and looked at it. "Before I came onboard I was not accustomed to eating for any reason other than to fill nutritional needs. The idea of eating something because it tastes good is still a new concept for me. The idea of eating because I am hungry, rather than because I am instructed, is also new."

"Sad way to live," Padalmo said, shaking his head. "If you ask me, life is about enjoying the little things. Food. Games." Moses saw something strange in Padalmo's expression. "A soft bed. Try it."

PROPHET OF THE GODSEED

Moses stared at the fruit for a few seconds, pondering whether he would like it or not. Its wrinkled skin unsettled him.

"What are you waiting for?" Padalmo said. He took a bite out of his own fruit.

"What if I don't like it?"

"So what? Don't eat it again."

Moses sighed. "Okay." He took a bit from the fruit, and found his mouth immediately filled with saliva. As he chewed the leathery fruit casing, a tartness mixed with sweetness filled his mouth. He swallowed quickly. "Sweet?"

"See? Good, right?"

"Too strong."

"You should try one on the vine, then. A bit more watery, if also a bit tart."

"I'll keep it in mind," Moses said, and put the little fruit down.

"*Moses.*"

"Yes, Anders," Moses said in English to his communicator. Padalmo looked at him curiously.

"*Do you have our guest with you?*"

"I do. I am in the mess with him. What do you need?"

"*I thought you were supposed to keep him in medical.*"

"The captain said to feed him if he was hungry."

"*I think she meant to feed him in medical.*"

"He didn't like the food I brought him."

Moses could hear an audible guff from Anders. *"Bah, doesn't matter. Dad wants to see him. In person. You still willing to do your talking trick with him?"*

"Of course."

"Make sure your uniform is in order. I'll be headed your way in a few minutes."

"What was that about?" Padalmo said after a moment.

"We have an important meeting after lunch," Moses said, smiling nervously.

***

Travole looked at the screen of his mobile positioning system. The faint spot of light indicating the far-off beacon of Padalmo had disappeared in the previous cycle and not returned. He had not slept as he thought he would, his decision now irreversible.

Perhaps if I had gone anyway, he thought. *We might not have come back here, but we could have gone somewhere.* He thought of his wife and child, and then sighed.

"Still looking morose, I see." It was Fala, one of the Highlord's younger wives. He felt a chill as her icy blue eyes watched him pocket his small screen. She walked across the wide waiting room, filled with comfortable benches, and stopped to look at an old painting.

"It's just my way," Travole said.

"Nonsense," Fala said. "Are you awaiting a task from Imalmo?"

So familiar with his name, Travole thought. "Yes. I cannot speak of the details. You understand."

"I understand if you do," Fala said. She sat down beside him. Her long dress flowed over her knees in a way that caught Travole's eyes. She leaned forward and he glanced at her breasts. Her hand moved and rested lightly on his leg, and Travole stiffened.

He remembered with deep guilt what they had done, when she had presented the great sum for his betrayal of his friend. The sex then had been the sealing of a contract, a way of guaranteeing to Fala that Travole would not reveal the plot to dispose of Padalmo to the boy's father, Imalmo. Now, he looked at the gestures of Fala with a mixture of lust, disgust, anxiety, and fear.

Fala stood up and walked to a darkened hallway. She paused and leaned against the corner and looked again at Travole with a gaze that beckoned him to follow. A slight smile parted her lips.

"When is your briefing?"

"Half a turn," Travole said. He felt his heart racing, and his mouth felt dry.

"Plenty of time. Come," she said and turned down the hall.

Feeling the oppressive guilt of a betrayer and a philanderer, Travole pushed his suddenly heavy body up and followed. He thought again of his wife and was disgusted with himself, but pushed as best he could her image out of his mind. Once the betrayal had been made, it was made. There was nothing to do but continue.

He followed Fala down the dim hallway to a square of light that he knew was one of the reclining rooms in the administrative wing of the palace. The sun shone inside at a skewed angle, providing an ideally comfortable dim light. A window looked out across the bay, but was positioned at an angle that still provided seclusion. Once Travole entered, Fala closed the door and locked it.

The room was full of knee-height seats and backless couches. With a swift motion, Fala removed her dress and laid herself down on a long leather-covered couch. And so, once again, Travole dug himself deeper into guilt and debt.

MEMORY:
Simple Tasks

15 months earlier, ship time

A<small>NDERS SIGHED</small>. Randall walked out of his office, attempting to look calm and unaffected, but stomped the way he always did when he felt internally frustrated. Anders closed off his task window and stood. His language matrix, one of the few things that he had been able to consistently concentrate on the last month, would have to wait for another time. He exited his office and took the lift down to the open storage area that housed most of the bulkier things onboard of *Icarus*.

Moses was there, shuffling around with his head down. He dragged around to his side a statically charged broom, sweeping in random circles and directions, doing little more for the piles of debris, dust, and dead human skin than creating a thin layer of it throughout the cabin.

"Moses," Anders said. Moses kept his bald head down. "Moses!" Anders said loudly, and tapped him on the shoulder. Moses flinched and dropped the broom. Anders bent down and picked it up, then handed it back to Moses, who regarded it curiously.

"Sweep?"

"Yes, Moses, sweep," Anders said. "You're doing a terrible job at it." Moses gazed at him with less than full understanding, seemingly unmoved. A dim light blinked on one of the implants on his head that the doctor didn't want to remove.

"How?"

Anders grunted in frustration. "You push all the dust into one place. Over here." Anders pointed to the dust collection inlet in the base of the wall. "Hit this switch, and it sucks it up."

Moses put the broom down and dragged it along the floor to the flat inlet, then hit the button. The dust was sucked up. A long streak in the dust was now visible on the flat floor. Anders pulled at his hair. The voice of his father came back to him. *He is like a child, Anders. We cannot cast him away now.* He took a deep breath.

"Let me show you." Anders took the broom gently from Moses and walked to the edge of the room. He swept from the corner in a succession of quick strokes, creating a pile of dirt as the dust rose and was sucked onto the broom. "Now you do it." He held out the broom and Moses took it. He imitated the short strokes, but didn't seem to realize that the point was to make a pile of dust.

"Push that pile," Anders said. "Sweeping is about moving all the dirt into one location for easy pickup by the filtration system. Just try going over spots you haven't done yet, pushing the dust into this pile. Good." Moses started to push the dust in a more orderly fashion, but would sometimes spread it all back out again. Slowly and carefully, Anders guided the simple man as he pushed the dust over to the collection inlet, forcing patience into his voice when his inner mind felt nothing but frustration and regret.

Moses paused as he got the first pile to the inlet and looked at Anders. Anders forced a smile, and for the first time since he had come on board, Moses smiled back.

CHAPTER 3
Macbeth

Malcolm Macbeth was a man whose physical presence did not demand respect; it commanded it. It was not his height, which was average; even his son Anders stood half a head taller than him. He was vital for a man over sixty, but not unnaturally so. He was healthy, but he was not as robust as a younger man. His hair was thick, but grey throughout. His age held but the memory of a good-looking man, hidden behind years of care and sorrow. His intellect, when it showed itself, was overwhelming, but he held it over no one.

For most people that came into Malcolm's presence the respect was born of experience beyond age; the experience of *ages*. He had overseen the birth of countless human worlds, first with his father and then, for as long as virtually any history on any world could recall, by himself as chieftain of the Macbeth clan, eternal travelers of the stars. His eyes held the birth and death of billions of people. It was, for most, like stepping into the presence of a god.

Yet, for those in the fleet, there was more than respect. Virtually every person onboard *Icarus* and its many semi-autonomous sections was related in some, immutable way to him. To those who grew up on the ship-fleet, he was the patriarch. For those that were recruited planetside for a voyage into the stars, he was the living ancestor of the clan's seeded holdings in the galaxy. He was not distant to his crew. He knew them, and loved them, like a father. When they erred, they feared not just his wrath or the bringing of naval discipline, but worried most about disappointing their parent.

It was this fear, of disappointing the man that had given him new life, that Moses felt when Macbeth entered the small conference room, his figure blocking out the bright stars in the window just past the door. Claribel and Anders, who sat in chairs on the opposite side of the table from Moses, stood up when the chieftain walked in, and Moses hastily followed suit.

"Good to see you all," Macbeth said, his face remaining calm. He took a seat at the end of the table and leaned in, folding his hands. Moses followed Claribel and Anders back down into the high-backed chairs. The table's glass-like top reflected stars around the shadow of Macbeth.

"You didn't bring Tully with you?" Moses said impulsively. He could sense a reaction from Anders and Claribel. Sighs? He couldn't put a finger on it.

Macbeth cracked a smile. "No, Moses. You can open a channel with her whenever you like though.

Just make sure you talk to Anders first." He dropped his smile and looked around the table. "Well, Status?"

Anders spoke up first. "We've made some headway into having an accurate translation matrix for the planet's current standard language. There are also at least a dozen secondary languages, and as many regional dialects of the primary language. We're ignoring those as best we can. They're internet is not standardized, either."

"There are two internets planetside," Moses said. Macbeth turned to him and raised an eyebrow. Moses looked at Anders. "Sorry for interrupting. Just something I picked up from the planetsider."

"We should have a working matrix within the standard day," Anders went on. "Until then, Moses has found a way to translate on the fly, and he's probably our best resource until we get our own systems online."

"He's also developed a bit of a rapport with our guest," Claribel said. "Who is in good health and decent spirits, by the way. I'm afraid I've had to go through Moses to gather any cultural information."

"What have you learned?" Macbeth said.

"You should probably ask Moses. He's the most in the know at the moment," Claribel said.

"I will," Macbeth replied. "Just give me a starting point. Moses is still learning to judge which details are important and which ones are not."

Claribel nodded and glanced at Moses. "The society below exists in many factions, dominated mostly by city-states. Of these, there are two primary military alliances, divided by religion, of sorts. Even their internets are separate, which I found notable."

"One of these internets is capable of interfacing with Moses's implants, correct?" Macbeth said. He brought up a screen on the top of the table and began flipping through files with his fingertip.

"Yes," Claribel said. "The faction that occupies most of the cold territories on the dark side of the planet has a more extensive network, with much broader interfacing capabilities. Moses's compatibility appears to be a coincidence, partly enabled by his implants' wide broadcasting frequencies."

"A most fortuitous coincidence," Macbeth said. He brought up a picture of part of the planet's habitable zone, rich and green but lit as if in dusk.

"The two religious factions have opposing dogma in regard to the progression of technology," Claribel continued. Screens lit up in the table below each of them, showing what Macbeth was perusing. "One faction opposes the use of implant technology, preferring to keep human interface devices as separate analogs."

"The wiser of the two, of course," Anders said.

"The other discounts these religious tenants as foolish, and permits full research. They wage war on one another over this. It is a limited war, for now."

"I can confirm," Anders said. "We have found through penetrating scans some one hundred million cybernetically interfaced individuals, all linked into the more expansive of the two internets."

PROPHET OF THE GODSEED

"Worrisome," Macbeth said. "And Tully and I have found our own pieces to worry about. Moses? What about our guest?"

"Our guest's name is Padalmo," Moses said. "He is one of many children from a family that rules a city in the habitable zone. He was in the desert attempting to complete a religious trial of some sort. His people apparently have some respect for it."

"Tell me about this man's people," Macbeth said.

"Anders was able to help me understand some details," Moses said, looking to Anders.

Anders nodded. "They engage in polygamy and polyamory in the higher castes especially. I conjecture it is an adaptation to perpetual war, which serves as a status generator in their society but also creates an artificially high male mortality rate, leaving a great many unattached females. The war, as Claribel said, is mostly religious. Their religion is of great importance. They have few names for their enemies. 'The Unfaithful' is the primary."

"You are proving yourself unexpectedly useful, Moses," Macbeth said. He looked out the window at the stars. "Unexpected at least in the means of use."

"Sir, there is something that I deem important for you to know," Moses said. Macbeth turned back casually. "Their religious texts are written in English, though they have forgotten how to speak it properly. They are composed, to a large degree, of the charter directives of the Macbeth clan, from when the planet was seeded some twelve years ago, standard ship time. You wrote the equivalent of their bible, sir."

Macbeth nodded calmly at the revelation that had seemed so large in Moses's mind. This was the man that Padalmo would look at like a god, and he seemed not to care.

"Sir?" Moses said. "Does that not... intrigue you?"

Macbeth smiled. "Would you believe that something like this is not only unsurprising, but a bit expected as well?"

"I would believe it," Moses said, "but mostly because you said it."

Macbeth chuckled. "I appreciate the trust." He rapped his knuckles on the table. "Teaching requires patience." He looked warmly at Moses. "Do you know much about the man I named you after?"

"Yes, he was a prophet to a tribe of people known as Hebrews on my home planet. He was saved by being drawn from the water as an infant."

"As we have drawn you, though I daresay you are no longer an infant," Macbeth said. "Moses was more than just a prophet. He was the founder of the Hebrew religion, their nation. He was given the Ten Commandments by God, and performed acts that were miraculous to those who witnessed them. Imagine that we took Moses from his wanderings in the desert and placed him before his descendants thousands of years later. How would people treat him?"

PROPHET OF THE GODSEED

"They would revere him," Moses said. "They would revere him like a god."

"That is what it is like when I return to a seeded world. When *we* return to a seeded world." The chieftain looked to his children at the table. "Moses compiled much of the Torah. He handed the Hebrews their law. He in many ways founded their culture. So do we, when we populate a planet, also plant the seed of their society. Its culture becomes the growth of what we have begun. Just as if Moses were to return to his children centuries later, we have returned to our children to find them very different. What do you think of that?"

Moses looked at the stars in thought for a moment. "We are not gods, sir."

"No, we are not," Macbeth said. "But even if we were gods, a god may create, and destroy, but that which is created has life of its own. These people are unique, something other than designed, as it is on all worlds. Do we play God?"

"I suppose we must leave them to their fate," Moses said.

"That's not what I said," Macbeth said. "We must tread lightly, or we may sweep away everything they have become. Everything that is unique. Our journey here, however, was not without purpose. We seeded this planet for a particular reason, and it was not to experience the growth of societies."

Moses frowned, disturbing his normally placid face. "Sir, what is that reason?"

Claribel spoke up. "This planet has a deceptively rich cache of stable heavy elements, including element 120. I know we haven't begun to train you in physics yet, especially not graviton physics, but suffice it to say that these isotopes are invaluable in the acceleration of our ships during interstellar travel."

"Valuable enough to seed a relatively hostile world to gain access to it," Macbeth said. "We are a little late collecting on what is owed us. Keep that reason in mind when we talk to our planetsider."

***

The air in the room felt still, despite the steady flow of the air circulators. The lights were dim, making the stars of night shine brightly through the large windows of corundum. The planet of Terranostra was inside a large nebula, left behind by the death-throes of an incredibly immense star. Though the nebula was invisible when you travelled inside it, it was a healthy star nursery with numerous close dwarf stars that filled the black spaces with hints of red light.

Padalmo sat on a grey chair, upholstered in the hide of a long-dead animal. He leaned on his knees with his elbows, staring at his hands as if afraid to lift his eyes and meet the gaze of the man who stood before him. Moses sat on a nearby couch, leaning close to the man as if to whisper. Claribel and Anders sat on another couch, datapads held in their laps. Their fingers worked quickly over silent and invisible keypads.

Malcolm Macbeth stood in the center, his legs relaxed. He held a datapad on his right forearm, and was cuing quickly through information. He looked up at Padalmo, who was rubbing his hands lightly.

"My name is Malcolm Macbeth." The chieftain looked at Moses and said. "Translate." Moses spat out some strange words.

Padalmo looked up to meet Malcolm Macbeth's eyes. The young man's own blue eyes trembled, and his mouth fell open. A few words spilled out. Malcolm looked to Moses, who translated.

"Then you are the Seeders."

"We brought people to your world, it is true." Malcolm nodded at Moses, who continued to translate, establishing the dialogue between the patriarch and the would-be prophet. "I hope you find the truth in our position self-evident." He gestured to the open bay of windows.

Padalmo fell out of the chair and onto his face. "I am not worthy to be your prophet, lord."

"It is not your place to decide worthiness," Macbeth said. "Nor am I tasking you with the burden of prophesy just yet. I am here to have a conversation. Please sit down."

The boy hesitated and pushed himself back into the arm chair. Macbeth pulled up a similar one, upholstered with a different, unfamiliar animal skin. He sat down and looked calmly at Padalmo. "It has been a long time since we have been here, Padalmo. Your people have grown and changed. I thank you for holding true to the directives I established so long ago."

"Not all of us have adhered to them, lord. There are many who no longer believe."

"And you fight them."

"Yes, but the conflict cannot go on forever."

"Who do you think will win?"

"We will. You will save us, lord."

"If we did not? If we let you fight your own war?"

"It is *your* war, lord, but if you did not end it, I see the unfaithful gaining victory. Soon. Their heresy has given them power, power beyond what we were meant to have, and it will be the end of us. *You must help.*"

Macbeth looked to Claribel, who slightly widened her eyes.

"Padalmo," Macbeth said. "I want to understand the strife of my children."

"They are not your children," Padalmo said, gritting his teeth. "They have forgotten you."

"That changes nothing," Macbeth said. "They are still people." He looked to Claribel. "They are still *people*, yet."

"As you say, lord."

"Tell me the story of your world, as you know it," Macbeth said. "It has been such a long time for me. Please. Tell me how it started, and how it will end."

"You want me to give you the history of the world?"

"As it concerns you and your people, yes."

Padalmo looked around with wide eyes.

*

PROPHET OF THE GODSEED

The cycle repeats. It is prophesied. The cycle will stop when we cease to resist the ever-marching forces of the disbelievers. We can slow it, but if we wish to persist as a world, as a people, we cannot disengage from it.

This cycle is explained in the Cha'tear, the holy book, but to understand the cycle, you must understand God, as unfathomable as he is.

God, the Creator, made all worlds, both harsh and beautiful. He created people, so that the worlds might be experienced and loved, but the nature of men and women was perverted in secret by the Adversary. The Adversary placed in the minds of men a seed of discord, of disobedience, of disbelief. This flaw would, however, not manifest in a man apart from his fellows, but a man whose mind would be dominated by the adversary. By seeking to rebel from the teachings of the Creator, he would become enslaved to the mind of the adversary. The free will imparted by God, the freedom to rebel, ends in the loss of the world to utter dominion of evil.

The Adversary is not the Creator. He has created no worlds. He has created nothing. Once men fall under the dominion of the Adversary, they lose the will God has given them, and so the world, once growing and changing, becomes stagnant. The adversary does not understand men, but God does, for they are made in his image. Creators.

God also made for man servants and guardians, the Seeders. They were like to men, but immortal, powerful, and immune to the taint of the adversary. God tasked them with the spread of his people, the God Seed, to the innumerable worlds amidst the heavens. They obeyed, and so Creation is understood and experienced by man. He also tasked the Seeders with preservation of mankind. By spreading the God Seed over countless worlds, made accessible only through the seeders, he prevented the spread of the Adversary's taint. That eternal opponent to God's dynamic change has conquered other worlds, it is said, but the seeders have halted what would encompass all creation. The defense of our world, however, is in the hands of man. The faithful resist, even now, but the cycle offers proof of our past failure, and redemption for the future if our strength does not hold.

The cycle, as we understand it, occurs between the forces of the faithful, those who respect the limits handed to them by the seeders, and the apostates, those who reject such limits, and seek power for themselves. They do not believe that the power they seek will eventually enslave them. That power, as the seeders have passed to us, is the growth of bond between man and machine. When machine becomes fully integrated with the man, the man is lost, and becomes a servant of the machine. Machines, meant to be servants, become masters, just as the Adversary, a servant of the Creator, wishes to make the Creator a servant to himself.

Temptation is strong. Once it plants its seed, it grows. Inevitably, it grows beyond the ability of the faithful to contain it, and the cycle must be reset. Servants must be destroyed, but for man and machine that are one, they both must be swept away. God destroys the world. A few faithful are chosen to remain and rebuild, but the seeds of the adversary can never be destroyed, but grow anew after each fire.

After the fire we rebuild the world, according to the will of God, preserving the dictates of the Seeders. We have done this, at least once. The world was consumed, but Podastamu, the first profit, was spared. He and his chosen were protected in a shelter amid Drogathalum, the Sea of Sand. After years of time, when the fire had burned away all life, the prophet emerged and put his followers to task in rebuilding south of the sunward side of Terranostra. Among them were seven priests, who came to found the seven dynasties. One of them, Daldalmo, was my ancestor, and founded the house of Tala'Drag'Chu, which rules the land surrounding the fifth holy city of Pana'Chu.

There have been many prophets since Podastamu, who have overseen the articles of faith, but of the seven dynasties, now only five remain. The other two have been swept away with the growth of the apostates from the dark side of the world. Their people turned away from God, ignored the words of the Seeders, and soon they found their houses in jeopardy. They were too late in responding, and the unfaithful unseated them in favor of new oligarchs who valued the rebellion of the Adversary.

We have fought them for generations, holding them at bay, destroying what capacity they have to unite with their machines, what should only be their tools. However, the tide is turning. The third city fell when I was a boy, and even Pana'Chu is not safe from sorties. We stand now on the precipice of another rebirth, when the cycle will have to begin anew.

I am the new prophet. I accept this now. I am not perfect, but I understand and trust fully in the directives of the Seeders.

*

Malcolm Macbeth sat leaning forward in a chair near to Padalmo. His palms were pressed together as his elbows rested on his knees. His fingertips were tensed against those of the opposite hand, held in front of a flat, calm face.

"Thank you for telling me this," he said. He waited for Moses to translate. "I have some more to ask, if you are willing to speak."

"I am always willing to speak to the seeders, or listen," Moses said, translating Padalmo's strange speech, laden with glottal stops.

"What directives do you hold from the holy texts?"

"Sir, you would know them better than I. You created them, did you not?"

"I did, but my question was not to what they say, but to what you hold. What things do you do to keep with the charter?" He shook his head and corrected himself. "Holy texts." He looked to Moses, who wore a worried look as he translated and listened for Padalmo's reply.

"We hold that technology should not be mated with man. That such a pairing will be the downfall of all of us, and we must act to prevent it. We hold that each man should have skills and specialties of his own, and that machines and computers should be tools of action, never of knowledge."

"Sounds close enough," Anders said, "though a bit fussied up, like in a bible."

"What about the purpose of the charter?" Macbeth said, sitting up. "What about the task set to you? I don't mean the restrictions we advised."

Padalmo looked confused as the translation came in. He shook his head. "I thought that was our task. Stopping the progress of the adversary."

Macbeth sighed and looked to Anders. "Something is missing, or not right." He glanced at Moses, who was beginning to recount the words in Padalmo's language. "Don't translate this." Moses nodded. "The mining directive was explicitly in the charter. We provided the facilities, and the tools. Could that have been lost, when so much else of the charter was enshrined?"

Anders looked at Claribel for a moment. "We didn't find any evidence of stable heavy element mining. They mine mundane things."

"They view the charter as a religious text," Claribel said. "They don't understand English anymore. Perhaps some of it got lost in translation."

"I have a thought," Moses said.

"Go on," Macbeth said.

"If the charter is a religious text now, perhaps they view it like other religious texts. Maybe they think what it says is... that one thing is meant that is different from what is said." Moses shook his head. "Sorry, I don't quite know how to say it."

"Metaphor," Anders said. "Maybe they thought mining was a metaphor for something."

Macbeth pursed his lips. "Moses. Translate." Moses nodded. "Tell me, prophet, how have your people succeeded in the recovery of rare earth elements?"

Padalmo looked confused. Macbeth sighed.

"Here," Claribel said, and handed her datapad to Malcolm. "It's a copy of the charter from the seeding, including relative values of heavy elements for seeding services."

Moses poured over the text, flipping through screens quickly. "Tell me, prophet, have you yet mined 500 tons of stable heavy elements, with at least 150 tons of the assemblage to be serviceable element 120?"

Padalmo opened his eyes wide. Moses translated, "I don't know how to answer that."

"Answer the only way you can, then."

"There is much disagreement over that passage, and I am no expert on the text. Truly, I do not know what it means."

"What does it mean to you?"

"I go with the classic scholars, then," Padalmo said. "The reference to elements that do not exist is meant to inspire man to perfection of his soul, and though the task is impossible, we are called to the effort nonetheless."

"Bloody hell," Macbeth said, and pushed himself up and out of the chair. He stomped toward the door. "Thank you for your answers," he said, turning back to look at the scared planetsider. "Claribel, you are with me. Anders, I'll leave you and Moses to our guest."

The door opened and Malcolm stepped out, cursing under his breath as he went.

MEMORY:
Twins Across Two Times

One year earlier, Ship time

ANDERS MACBETH waited at what he presumed to be the analogue of a café. The patio was ringed in verdant foliage of some unknown variety, and filled with people speaking in the strange accent typical of Rondella Duo. It was still English, old and proud, but it had a sick, throaty quality to it that Anders disliked. It sounded to him like a croaking of some cadre of amphibious creatures, and did nothing to aid his anxiety.

"Here you go, dolly-wa," his waitress said in her strange tone, and dumped a wide cup of a mocha-brown liquid in front of Anders.

"Thank you." Anders looked up with a smile. The waitress smiled back sweetly. *At least that gesture never changes from world to world, or age to age,* he thought. "You must forgive me, but do I pay you now, or at the end of our exchange?"

"Bully, you daft?" She closed an eye, but kept smiling. Her hair was arranged so that it made dozens of product-stiffened blonde points around the top of her skull. It seemed at odds with the simple beauty of her unadorned face.

"Also," Anders went on. "Are galactic trade credits acceptable?"

"I gets it," the waitress said, and pointed upward. "You're from elsewhere." Anders nodded. "Pay when you like. Have to ask the boss 'bout credits." She looked him over. "My, but you're cute, dolly-wa." She shook her head and ambled away. Anders let himself watch her body move under a loose robe that seemed to hug only her hips.

He took a sip of the drink and realized right away it was not coffee. It was cold and powerfully bitter, but before he could spit it back in the cup, the taste changed to sour, and finally sweet. He looked at the brown liquid again. He took another sip, and this time held it in his mouth. It became even sweeter.

"Interesting," Anders said to himself, watching the sway of the waitress as she walked from table to table. "Must change taste as it gets warmer."

"It's actually a bitter starch reacting with your salivary amylase." Anders looked up to see his twin sister Claribel standing behind him, just to his left. He put down his cup and stood up in a hurry. She drew him into a quick hug. She released and gave him a warm smile. "It's good to see you."

"It's good to see you too," Anders said. He looked over his sister. It was definitely Claribel. Her eyes were the same pure blue as his own, though they were now crowded by crow's feet and fine lines. She wore the same smile as when they were children, but it was now framed by laugh lines pulling on skin that had grown

PROPHET OF THE GODSEED

slightly loose. Her hair, once striking blonde, now held little of its former gold, fading to grey. She still wore it long and loose about her shoulders, the vanity of her youth now a piece of pride in her old age.

"How long has it been?" She said, sitting down. She flagged over the waitress.

"Galactic standard years? Some fifty-five hundred," Anders said. "Ship's clock, about five ancestral years."

Claribel nodded. "How old are you now?"

"We celebrated my twenty-ninth a few weeks ago," Anders said. "You?"

"Sixty. I'll be sixty-one in about a month." The waitress came and put another mug of the brown liquid in front of Claribel, who smiled kindly at her.

"That's almost as old as da'!" Anders said, then added with a smile, "Well, you don't look it."

"I see that you're still a terrible liar," Claribel said, and sipped her drink. "Half a percent loss of velocity makes a hell of a difference when approaching light speed, eh?"

"Yeah," Anders said. "We're working on another engine upgrade right now. Getting a few ticks closer to the limit."

"I know. I'll be overseeing some of the modifications."

"What?" Anders said, gulping down the bitter drink before it could become sweet.

Claribel gave Anders a forced smile. "I'm coming back on board the ship-fleet."

Anders leaned forward. "You are? That's great news, but why?"

"Masahiko died about two years ago," Claribel said. "I know our communications have been sparse..." She looked at her drink.

"I'm sorry," Anders said. He reached a hand out and touched hers. The skin felt different than he remembered. "Masahiko was a good man, or I wouldn't have let him take you away from us."

"We are powerful, Anders. All the spacing clans are, but we cannot turn away the inevitability of death. I have accepted it. Now is the time to think of the future."

Anders nodded. "Almost forty years with the Hosokawa clan... that's more than you spent with us. You willing to just walk away? Leave all those connections behind?"

"The Hosokawa accepted me and respected me," Claribel said. "But I have no children. I have lived as a Hosokawa, and contributed to their prosperity, in my own way. I could be very powerful among the fleetship, even without my husband, but ultimately, I will always be a Macbeth."

"Well, it will be good to have you back," Anders said, and raised a cup. "Shall we keep your birthday as the same day as mine, or move it backward?"

"I prefer chronological accuracy," Claribel said, raising her own cup. "But of course, an old woman never cares to be reminded of her age in any event."

PROPHET OF THE GODSEED

"Good, I never liked sharing a birthday with you. You gathered far too much of father's attention."

"And you gathered too much of mother's"

"Not anymore."

Claribel's face went downcast. "I know. I'm sorry."

"Think nothing of it," Anders said, and clanked his cup against his sister's.

They both drank.

The waitress approached again. "Just wanted to let you know that my shift is ending, but we're staying open during the shadow hours, and we have a few specials."

Anders looked up in the sky as she flitted away, and realized the sun had been growing dimmer.

"This part of Rondella Duo has a daily eclipse. Lots of people use it to take naps. At least, they did the last time I was here," Claribel said.

"How long ago was that?"

"I think our waitress's great-great-great grandmother was probably still in diapers."

Anders chuckled. "Did they always drink this stuff?"

"On this continent, at least." Claribel shuffled the half-empty cup in her hands. "Listen, there's something you should know. Father offered me a captainship."

"He did?"

"Greywing," Claribel said. Anders sat silently. "I know that's your ship-wing, and you probably had your eye on it."

"You obviously have more experience. It's fine. Expected, really."

"I told you that you're a bad liar," Claribel said. She looked at her cup. "Something about this slop. Goes right through me." She stood up. "That or I'm just getting old. I'm going to go see if I can find a bathroom. Say a prayer that this culture still uses knee-high toilets and gives a woman some privacy." She smiled and walked back to the building adjacent to the wide patio.

Anders watched her go. She still felt like his sister, but she seemed very different, in more than just age. She seemed... worn.

"I think it's sweet to take your mother out for a cup." Anders turned to look at the waitress. She seated herself where Claribel had just been and rested her face on a hand. "No nice chaps like you around here anymores. My mother said I should find a man who respects his own."

"She's actually my sister," Anders said.

"Your father's got quite the loin, then."

"That he does."

"All the same. I get off here in a few minutes. You going to stay up? You said you aren't from here; if you need a spot to sleep, I got a pad nearby. What do you say, dolly-wa?"

Anders had to stop from shaking his head at the proposition. "Thanks for the offer, but-"

"I'm Iwata. What's your name?"

Anders smiled. "Anders. Anders Macbeth."

PROPHET OF THE GODSEED

"Now you're bulling," the waitress said, and stood up. "If you didn't like me you could have just said so."

Anders withdrew a small datapad from his pocket and handed it to the waitress. "If you are leaving, I probably ought to pay you. All the financial info should be on there. You can just put the whole café's tab on there, if you like."

"Pah!" The waitress said, and ambled off.

Anders looked up at the darkening sky, growing to a pale shade of green as the moon began to move into the path of the sun.

***

Anders heard his door chime. He pulled his eyes away from the window, through which he watched the slow turning of Rondella duo.

"It's me." He recognized the voice of his father.

Anders flicked over a control screen next to his chair and unlocked the door. "Come in."

"You took your time getting back." Malcolm Macbeth settled into the chair opposite and looked out the window at the water-filled planet below. A round dark shadow cast by the planet's moon hung in the middle of it.

"I wanted to see at least a few sights."

"You sure you weren't spending your time indoors?"

Anders smiled at his father. "You talked to Claribel."

"I did, but not about you. Perhaps I just know my son," Malcolm said. Anders nodded. "Was it an arcade, or a woman?"

"A woman, but I discovered that sleep – and I mean sleep, father – is a rather casual social experience in this culture. It's like having a drink to them." Anders sighed and looked at his father. "Are you upset with me?"

"I'll not tell you how to live your life, other than how it pertains to the ship and the clan." Malcolm looked out the window for a few seconds. "Claribel wanted to come back. With Randall's decision to stay planetside on Delinda, I have need of a level-headed, experienced commander."

"I don't fault your judgment," Anders said. "Claribel was always smart and capable, and now she has experience. Almost as much as you do."

"It will be strange having my daughter as a peer," Macbeth said. A silence settled in and they both turned their eyes to the planet.

"Would I have been ready for command if Claribel had not wished to return?" Anders said, not looking at his father.

"No."

"Because of what I did with Moses?"

"Yes."

"I saved a life, father. It was the right thing to do."

"Yes, it was."

Anders turned to look at him. "Then why punish me? You tell everyone onboard to think independently, and then you punish me when I do exactly what you say you expect."

"I ask you to *think* independently, not *act* independently. Your job as a commander is not to do whatever you think best, even if it *is* best. Your job is to convince me of the correct course, and remain open to convincing yourself. When you defy orders and act on your own, you put the clan at risk, those under your command at risk, and undermine the social structure that keeps our family functioning."

Anders remained silent as Malcolm stood up.

"I love you more than words, Anders. My responsibility to you is to make you into the best man you can be. That's not always an easy task, for either of us, but I want to leave this clan in good hands. I have no doubt you will live up to my expectations." He gripped Anders on the shoulder. "When you're done moping, we're having a welcoming party for Claribel in the Greywing mess."

Anders nodded, and continued staring out the window.

CHAPTER 4
The Gate

Tully's face appeared warm and she wore a slight smile, despite the apparent bags under her eyes, and the com camera which tended to bleach out colors as it compressed data. She sipped a cup of coffee that Malcolm knew would be cold, but still much needed.

"Sorry to press you like this Tully," Malcolm said. He leaned back and pushed his hand through his grey hair, showing his granddaughter a soft side seldom seen by others in the fleet. "The military maneuvers planetside are beginning to heat up. Our time table might be shrinking."

The girl shrugged and took another sip of coffee from her colorful stonework mug. "If I'm not pressed, I'm bored to tears. Have you told the planetsider what's going on?"

"Not yet," Malcolm said. "I don't want to pervert his perspective with political motivations until we get a better grasp on what's happening."

"Which is?" Tully said.

"War is breaking out," Malcolm said. "I gather from Padalmo – that's the lad's name – that war is near constant here, but in limited sorties. Both alliances are beginning mass mobilizations."

"Not good," Tully said, almost absent-mindedly. "For us or them, eh?"

"No on both. Where are you on data reconstruction?"

"I'm through with logs and user-generated files," Tully said. "They should be transmitting to you. Operation code is being recovered and checked against the code we keep as backup for our quantum gates. It's pretty much all automated now."

"Good," Macbeth said. "Is there anywhere to sleep up there?"

"Egad, why would I want to try sleeping in this damn floating tomb?" She sneered.

"Because when you are done recovering code, I need you to get that gate back online."

Tully pushed her hair out of her face as she looked at another screen. "Okay then. I guess I can root around in the crew quarters. Life support is on."

"No second guessing?" Macbeth said, raising his eyebrows. "No asking why?"

"I'm sure the answer's not going to help me sleep." She sighed. "Let's see what a two-thousand year-old mattress feels like."

"Thanks, Tully," Macbeth said. "And if you check in the transport I think you'll find a self-inflating mattress. I'll be sending some more help in a few hours."

PROPHET OF THE GODSEED

*

Moses sat near Anders in the comfortable observatory room, watching Padalmo look wistfully out the window at his planet, sitting apparently motionless in space, one side pointed ever toward the sun beyond. Greywing lay in the shadow of the Terranostra, and looking at the planet from the dark side gave an interesting impression: a large, halo-like ring of light surrounded an interior that faded to black. Bright lights shone like beacons amid the frost of the dark side, a testament to the will and technological prowess of those Padalmo regarded as unfaithful.

Moses tuned out the many intersecting data streams that his cybernetic implants interacted with on the dark side. Peace and quiet returned to the ship, a state he had grown to like in his time with the Clan Macbeth, so different from the all-encompassing thoughtless noise of his origins. In silence, he felt like an individual, and only became aware of some recent loss of that feeling as the planetside transmissions faded away and his own wandering thoughts returned to him.

He became aware of Anders's eyes flitting over his datapad, sorting through information that his crawler program had deemed relevant on the planet's internets, fed through the translation matrix his unit had worked so hard to bring online.

"The chieftain told me I should talk to you about something," Moses said.

"What's on your mind?" Anders said, glancing up from his task.

"He said I should talk to you before opening a channel with Tully."

"Why?" Anders said. "Not against the rules as far as I know."

"I don't know why; he didn't explain. He just said I should talk to you first." Moses frowned. "Actually, he was the one who told me to open a channel, too."

Anders looked up, his hands pausing. "Are you attracted to Tully?"

Moses's frown deepened. "Attracted?"

"Do you think she's pretty?" Anders said, smiling slightly as he returned to his task.

"I don't know. How do I know if I think that?"

Anders chuckled. "This shouldn't be that hard. Do you like to look at her? More so than say, me?"

Moses scratched his chin. Like Anders, he was developing a short beard from a few days without much opportunity for personal hygiene.

"I guess I do," Moses said.

"Then you are probably attracted to her. It's quite normal."

"I also visualize her sometimes, when I don't have anything to do," Moses said. "I don't know why. I can usually steer my own thoughts, but sometimes I think of her impulsively."

"Yeah, you definitely have a crush on her," Anders said, smiling.

PROPHET OF THE GODSEED

"Is that what I need to know before opening a channel with her?" Moses said. Anders laughed aloud, and Padalmo turned back to look at him, his blue eyes wide.

"Well, first of all, you shouldn't open a channel with her. She's got too much going on right now. It would just make her mad."

"Alright, then. Thank you," Moses said.

"I'm not finished. Normally, when you are sexually – let's say romantically – attracted to someone, you pursue a relationship with that person."

"I already have a relationship with Tully. She is my secondary superior-"

"That's not what I mean. I mean a romantic relationship, like getting a girlfriend or a wife."

"Courtship."

"Yes."

"How do I get Tully to court me?"

"*You* don't." Anders looked up and smiled wryly. "Normally – I mean normally, mind you – you spend time with someone, then if you get the right signals, you express romantic interest. If those are returned, you enter a courtship period, which can last a highly variable amount of time. During that courtship period, you explore compatibility of different factors, and eventually, you decide on a life partnership."

"Marriage. I know all this."

"Do you? Because you're acting pretty damn clueless."

"I'm just trying to attach feelings to concepts, Anders."

Anders rubbed his brow. "I know, I'm sorry for being harsh and laughing at you."

"I forgive you," Moses said. He watched the planet for a few moments. "So you don't think Tully would court me?"

"You shouldn't pursue it, Moses. Tully is my niece, the chieftain's granddaughter. His only granddaughter, for the moment, and my father has an extremely soft place in his heart for her. Malcolm Macbeth is a well-controlled man, but if you want to see just how wrathful he can be, poke him in his one soft spot."

"Why did the chieftain have me talk to you?"

"I presume, to have me shoo you off of her."

"Thanks for speaking to me about this, Anders," Moses said.

"You're welcome," Anders said. He paused and looked at single data screen on his pad. He scrolled through it quickly. "I have an idea on some things to talk to Padalmo about. We can try out the translation matrix, too."

"So you won't need me," Moses said flatly.

"That's not what I said," Anders said. He stood up and walked over to the couch against which Padalmo leaned.

"Padalmo," Anders said. His datapad spat out a mechanical voice in the new language. "Would you please tell us about your prophet..." he flipped open

PROPHET OF THE GODSEED

his notes. "The place your prophet Podastamu hid from the destruction of the world."

Padalmo looked strangely at Anders. Moses quickly tuned his implants back into the frequencies of the planetary net, and repeated the question in Padalmo's language.

Padalmo smiled slightly at him. Moses caught Anders looking over at him with a raised eyebrow.

***

The screens lining the room lit the sunless interior with a bright cool light. Each screen contained the image of a great man, a highlord from each of the holy cities. Imad watched his father Imalmo stand at the center of the room. His older brother Dimlo reclined next to him, his military uniform looking like a casual suit on him. Imad noted how relaxed his brother looked, and so did his best to find the medium between his own anxiety and the outward uncaring of his brother. He sat up straight, but relaxed his face.

"What we need now, more than ever before in our time, is unity," Imalmo said. "The Darksiders are preparing a great attack. An invasion the likes of which we have not seen in two generations. If we each focus on holding our own lands we will be overwhelmed, one at a time."

"In ten generations, we have stood together as the faithful. What else is there?" One of the men on the screens, Pada'ark, the Highlord of Uldama, spoke. His stroked his white beard.

"We have recognized each other as faithful," Imalmo said. "But our alliance has been one of ideology only. Our resources we have not coordinated."

"Nonsense," another voice said. It was Malalko, the highlord of Jafta, a city rivaled in size and grandeur only by Pana'chu. "When have I ever refused a military contribution when asked? We have always supported each other."

"But only as separate armies, in our separate lands," Imalmo said. "Not as one fighting force. Never have any of our soldiers worked directly with the others. Never have we fielded a true force for conquest."

"Who would rule the conquered lands?" Fadasta spoke, the aging highlord of Pana'Gill. "Things are the way they are for a reason."

"Armies are made by us each in their own ways. Combining them would be chaos," Pada'ark said. "The men have allegiance only to their highlord. Grouping them together would only cause them to abandon each other to death. Old rivalries die hard, highlord."

"They do not have allegiance only to their highlord," Imalmo said.

"I think I see where this is going," Malalko said. "I have gathered recently that one of your sons has attempted the trial of the prophet, something that has not been completed in two generations. Has he returned?"

"He as not," Imalmo said. "Though I know now that tongues in my house are loose."

"We are not enemies," Malalko said.

"But we are rivals," said Pada'ark. "Be only upset when somebody does something that you do not."

Imalmo ignored the comment and continued. "My son has not returned, nor do I think he is likely to, but if a prophet were to arise, it would do a great deal for unifying the intent of our militaries. The question remains as to whom."

"Whoever completes the trial, of course," Malalko said.

"Ah, I understand," Pada'ark said. "Who better to head the faith than one of its caretakers?"

Imalmo raised an eyebrow. "Yes."

"Election has not happened in a terrible long count of years," Fadasta said. "Since even before the destruction of Pana'Tull."

"Election is heresy!" Malalko said. "You cannot be honestly suggesting that we deceive our men and put on a prophet of pretense while our enemies close in around us."

"There is no pretense," Imalmo said. He leaned forward and looked at Malalko's image with a hard, cutting gaze. "Just as Podastamu had to forge a new destiny, so shall we, if we hope to hold what is dear to us.

Imad flinched as Dimlo elbowed him. They locked eyes and Dimlo nodded off to the side. Imad followed his brother around a wall, out of sight of the monitors. Imalmo continued to talk to the men, and it seemed most of them were speaking well of the plan he was slowly, deftly, laying out.

"What is it?" Imad asked.

"Are you trying to get disowned?" Dimlo said. He grabbed Imad's lapels and pulled him close.

"What are you talking about?" Imad said.

"That scowl of yours," Dimlo said. "You shaking your head like that when father was talking about the plan. You realize those men can see that, right?"

"What?" Imad said, and realized that how he had felt listening to his father – guilt, anger, fear, and the sickness of one who is seeing his faith destroyed – he might have been showing physically as he watched the faces, so intent was he on the outcome of the meeting.

"Keep control of your damn emotions," Dimlo said. "Father never should have let someone so green into the inner circle. You've fought what, two battles?"

"Three," Imad said. "And I have as much right to be here as you."

Dimlo grimaced at him. "You slack your face next time we bring you into a meeting. You are there to demonstrate power, not discord, especially with this."

"I'm... I'm sorry, I didn't understand."

"Well I for one will not stand for this!" Malalko's voice boomed from the meeting chamber. "Consider our alliance ended!"

Dimlo released Imad. "See what you have contributed to. A man can be convinced of anything with the right presentation."

PROPHET OF THE GODSEED

Imad hung his head as Dimlo walked away.

***

Malcolm Macbeth flipped through more videos Tully had recovered from the quantum gate. Once the means by which instantaneous trade and transport with the other seeded worlds had enriched Terranostra, the Quantum gate was now a sepulcher, forsaken by the inhabitants of Terranostra, which had been left floating derelict in orbit above the planet for millennia. Images lit up his dark office, the stars behind giving the only other light in the packed space. A well-kept man spoke English in a familiar accent. He was talking about power surges.

Date codes had ceased to be entered in data and professional logs all at once, as if all systems had failed at the same time. Malcolm had tried to peruse the videos starting with the last date and working backward, looking for clues as to how the gate had been shut down, cutting Terranostra away from the rest of the galactic trade network in one, sudden strike. The video logs, however, were anything but conclusive.

For the most part the men and women who occupied the floating space station had been going about standard business, making notes about anomalies in the flux of space between the gates, making hypotheses about quantum entanglement research, or otherwise musing on traffic coming from other worlds. These were expected topics for Malcolm to see. Only the best and the brightest in a given world were tasked with caring for the quantum gates, the pinnacle of the spacing clans' technology, and their interests tended to be academic.

Malcolm sighed. He pinged Tully's com to see if she was awake. She was not. The door opened and Claribel stepped in.

"Any luck?" she said, stepping behind Malcolm's chair.

Malcolm rubbed the bridge of his nose. "Nothing. Just standard video logs. The crawler's gone through all the written data, even going back a few decades from shutdown. There was nothing to predict this. You?"

"We cracked the encryption on personal local storage and took a look at some of their video logs. Mostly diary stuff, occasional local copies of written and video transmissions to the planet. We've learned a lot. I'd love to pick Tully's mind."

"She's sleeping, and I'm not willing to wake her just yet. When she does wake, I plan on keeping her busy."

"Trying to reactivate the gate?"

"Yes," Malcolm said. "If we can't recover the resources we need, I want the option to leap back to a safe world for resupply."

"Expensive."

"We can afford it. What did you learn that was so interesting?"

Claribel turned a light on, very dim, illuminating Malcolm's workspace, which was crowded with trinkets surrounding an oversized terminal. She propped up her datapad and began flipping through notes.

PROPHET OF THE GODSEED

"Personal logs show that there was some conflict brewing below, political in nature. The crew of the gate was worried about it, and their families. Discussion about it becomes sparse leading up to what we are calling the cutoff date."

"What was the nature of the conflict?"

"Government restriction of data access, a push for planetary isolation, regional isolation, and territorial tensions. Most of all, there was worry about a particular political leader, who was building up a military arsenal."

She opened up a video. A young woman's face filled the screen.

"Hey mom, it's me," the woman said, in plain and understandable English. "I wanted to tell you to get out of Cummins. One of the men up here is from Panwarke, and he said that things are going bad in his home province. Communications are all being filtered through government channels, but he's managed to find out that chancellor Portalay has seized a huge number of private assets, including holdings of the Macbeth Corporation. What they call the "citizen's initiative" has been revealed for what it truly is – an attempt to control the populace through the use of cybernetic monitoring devices, all while they lock down the internet and cripple their people."

Malcolm watched as the young woman pushed a hand through her dark hair, trying to choke back tears. "He's going to attack. Jeffrey – that's my friend's name – is sure of it. Portalay knows seizing clan assets could cause an interplanetary war. He wants it. The worst part is, I don't know if anyone planetside understands just how dangerous a dictator he is. His curtain of control is pretty absolute in Panwarke. I know what I'm saying is crazy, or seems impossible, but I need you to trust me on this. We can see things up here in the gate you can't imagine.

"So please, mom, listen. Pack up what you need, get Pitt, and I know you don't get along, but please find dad, for me, and leave. Head somewhere out of the way. An ag zone, or some place you can stand to be up near the sun side. It doesn't really matter; I just don't want you in the capital for the next few deviations. I don't know if I'll have another chance to deliver a message that isn't being watched by Portalay's government, or our own. Please."

The young woman's head hung and she reached forward to end the recording.

"How close was this to the cutoff date?" Malcolm said.

"A month." Claribel pushed her hair out of her face and looked at the Chieftain.

"They must have thought their standard transmissions and logs were being monitored by this Portalay fellow. It explains the lack of interest leading up to the cutoff." Claribel sighed. "A despot, with a mind to rule the world. How often have we seen this repeat? I believe indeed that's what caused this, and sent the planet into a dark-age, from which they are only now truly recovering."

PROPHET OF THE GODSEED

Malcolm shook his head. "Conquerors don't obliterate that which they wish to rule. We're missing some piece that explains the end of this, including the deactivation of the gate."

"Interstellar war?"

"The holdings we have left on other planets have more than enough capacity to meet a military threat on this world."

"That may be true, but that doesn't mean the gate operators knew that. For all we know, they turned off the gate to protect the rest of the trade network."

Malcolm rubbed his forehead. "There were no human remains on the gate. Systems were mostly intact."

"What about logs without date codes?" Claribel said. "The date codes are automated by the active system, and synced to galactic standard time, which flows at different rates based on where you are in the galaxy, and gravity, and-"

"You're right; they could have kept making logs after the gate was deactivated. The clock would have been reading zero since the gate was closed." Malcolm snapped his fingers and brought his huge terminal display back to life.

Lines flashed across the screens, words flitted by, along with images, at a pace too fast for Claribel to discern one thing from another. Video previews flashed across the screen, then disappeared. Data logs flew across the screen. Malcolm's mind was moving at full speed.

"There's a treasure-trove of data here," the chieftain said. "But it's mixed up. Half of these entries are from when the gate was first built, prior to its linkage with the rest of the network, and the other half appears to be what we are looking for.

"There, that author," Claribel said, and pointed a finger at the display. Malcolm paused at a video file. "That's your call-sign, isn't it? What's that doing here?"

Macbeth nodded and cued up the video. "I must have made this twelve years ago, probably as a building log prior to activation."

The display leapt to life. They saw the inside of the control room of the quantum gate, the same place Tully had been working with Malcolm a day prior. The controls were bright and clean, with backlit buttons and keyboards spaced around crisp displays. Lines of data outputted on a central screen at the back of the room. Steel and titanium gleamed the way only something new can. A younger Malcolm Macbeth looked into the camera, his hair still a rich tan, only showing grey around his temples. He smiled as he leaned forward in his chair.

"Welcome. This station represents the fifth revision of my father's quantum gate design. Before I introduce you to our systems and explain their use, I wanted to explain a bit about the enhancements we have made in quantum entanglement technology. If you are an engineer from a previously seeded planet, as I expect most of you to be, you should notice some of these

PROPHET OF THE GODSEED

upgrades immediately. If you are a new trainee, try not to gloat when you talk to your counterparts in other systems."

"I made this video as a tutorial introduction," Malcolm said to Claribel as he watched the image of himself stand up and walk around the bay of terminals. "I must never have implemented it. It's amazing to see it new, just as it was twelve years – or two thousand years – ago."

The image of the younger Malcolm continued to talk, leaning against a rail. "We have, through hardware upgrades, enhanced the energy throughput to the next linkage, shortening the amount of time and power necessary to generate a hole through space-time. With our latest software revisions, we have also made the automation of basic systems more fluid, with a tighter and easier to read display that makes monitoring by the crew all the easier."

"There you are," a woman's voice said off the screen. Malcolm's image turned to look at it.

"Ah, that's why," Malcolm said as he watched. He reached for the keyboard to end playback, and found Claribel had stopped his hand.

"Wait, I think I remember this," she said. "I was seventeen."

A slim red-haired woman, looking middle-aged but lively, stepped into the camera's view. She held in her arms a plastic vessel with a flat bottom.

"I'm not interrupting, am I?" she went on.

"No," the younger Malcolm said. "I'll finish up later."

"I thought it would be fun to have the twins' birthday party onboard the gate. A little bit of a dual celebration, eh?" the woman said with a smile. She put down the vessel on a flat surface near the consoles and removed the top, revealing three small, well-decorated cakes. "One for Anders, one for Claribel, and one for you, to celebrate another success."

"That's mom," Claribel said, her eyes focusing intently on the screen.

The young Malcolm on the screen drew the woman into a deep kiss. She leaned backwards into his arms as he did so, then broke the kiss with a laugh. Malcom fast-forwarded through the footage.

"I'm sorry, da'," Claribel said. "I didn't think about how you'd feel."

"You lost her too, dear," Malcom said. He slowed the video back into normal time.

More voices filled the microphone, and a few more people stepped into the view of the camera. One was clearly Anders, though he was skinnier, and his hair was poorly combed. A tall and slim blonde girl stepped into frame, smiling.

"That's you," Malcolm said. "This was Anders and your eighteenth birthday." The blonde girl in the video hugged Malcolm. "My God, I remember looking at you and realizing you were an adult. A woman. It was upsetting." Malcom shook his head as he watched. "You started courting Sean after this. I nearly blasted that boy out of the airlock once. It's not easy to watch a daughter grow up."

"What about watching one grow old?" Claribel said.

Malcolm shrugged. "Twelve years. Feels like yesterday, at least this bit. You?"

"This was forty-three years ago, for me," Claribel continued. She sighed.

"I miss her," Malcolm said. "Your mother."

"Me too," Claribel said. "Sorry to tell you, it doesn't get any easier. I spent three decades travelling with the Hosokawa, and not a week went by that I didn't want her advice. I'm an old woman now, and I still want it."

The Malcolm on the screen looked at the camera, approached, and turned it off.

"We should get back to work," the current Malcolm said, bringing up more screens of videos. "Can you have data processing automate some searches so we can find the relevant written data logs?"

Claribel nodded. "Do me a favor and save that video, or anything else you find of her. Or us."

"I will," Malcolm said, focusing on the terminal display. Claribel walked out of the room, shutting out the light as she went. Malcolm slumped after the door closed and leaned on his desk. He brought up the video again, watching his wife hug and kiss him.

"Oh, Deidre," Malcolm whispered. He rubbed his temples. "Never can I escape you." The red-haired woman smiled at the camera. "Nor do I want to."

CHAPTER 5
Fires of the Past

"Tradition varies, of course," Padalmo said, trying to sound confident. As Moses translated to Anders, Padalmo looked out the window. The constant fear and wonder of awakening with the seeders was gradually yielding to a sense of calm and security. He had never seen his own planet from above, except perhaps in pictures retrieved from their communications satellites. Seeing the entirety of it live was a humbling experience. He watched storms move across the inhabitable zone, and thought it was like watching the world breath.

"According to your own tradition, where is the Fire Ark?" Moses said, after conferring with Anders in the holy language. Padalmo was still having trouble picking out the specifics, though he recognized a few words.

"No tradition is mine," Padalmo said. "Tradition is... tradition. There are different schools of thought, I suppose. Reformed practitioners believe that the entire concept of the Fire Ark to be metaphorical, and that Podastamu's sequestration was a spiritual, not physical, transformation. Most apologists wish to avoid the point all together, not wanting a search for evidence to complicate the pursuit of virtue in the now. Some think that faith should rule, the search itself is sacrilege. There are, however, researchers who strive to find the physical evidence for the story."

Padalmo pointed out the window as he continued talking. "Above the habitable zone, in the sunward side of Terranostra, is where the texts say that it is. There, in the *Karakûm*, Podastamu waited out the fire. That is why the trial of the prophet is in the desert. There have also been discoveries of structures, settlements, at the edges of the Karakûm, by the Barrier Mountains and near the steaming sea, which suggested people existed there for a short time. Nobody can live there now."

Padalmo watched Moses confer with Anders. He then said, "The Fire Arc was not found in these structures?"

"No," Padalmo said. "The ever-shifting sands of Drogathalum make finding any structure very difficult. The settlements we have discovered are in slightly more hospitable areas, but lack what should be the Ark. A rather infamous treasure hunter once said he found signs of a buried structure of iron and lead, using seismic information, but he could not find the spot again when put to task. The Fire Ark remains hidden."

"So it was made of iron?" Moses said.

"Yes, it was made of metal. That is what the books say, anyway."

PROPHET OF THE GODSEED

Moses nodded. "Could you point out this particular place? The place the treasure hunter was? Either from orbit or on a map?"

"Probably not. I don't take such searches seriously. Or, I didn't until now." Padalmo cocked his head. "Why would you need my help? It was the seeders that guided Podastamu's hand."

Moses and Anders shared some words, then Moses said. "We are deciding something, just a moment."

Padalmo heard the voice of Malcolm Macbeth, the legendary progenitor of the God Seed, through a device that Anders held. Anxiety crept up his spine as he heard the tone of the Macbeth, which was terse and full of anger. Impatience.

"Have I angered him?" Padalmo said.

Moses shook his head and continued listening to the progenitor talk. Finally, he and Anders turned back.

"Do you truly wish to be prophet?" Moses said. "You must think on this. There is a chance that you will not be permitted to return home, depending on how events go in the near future."

Padalmo did take a moment to reflect. He looked back out the window at the slowly breathing planet.

"I am already dead," he said. "That is what it means to walk into the desert. You must die to the world."

"It is why we saved you," Moses said. "To the world, you are dead. But is it dead to you?"

"No, but I am ready to serve."

Moses looked intently at him. "The chieftain believes that in order to be our prophet, you must know and understand the truth. Faith and comfortable beliefs will be challenged."

"I am prepared," Padalmo said.

Anders and Moses spoke some quick words. Moses nodded and activated a device that appeared to be all display, showing words that Padalmo recognized from copies of the holy texts.

"You call us the seeders, which is an appropriate name," Moses said. Anders spoke quickly beside him, so Padalmo could not be sure of who was saying what. "What we do is seed different planets with immense space between them. It may take many centuries for us to travel between worlds, though time does not pass the same to us as to you. Terranostra is one of these seeded worlds. Usually, a planet, once settled, is gifted with what we call a quantum gate. This is a device that allows near instantaneous communication and transportation between worlds.

"There is a quantum gate still in orbit above your world, but it was deactivated long ago. After conversing with you and probing your networks, we think that it was likely deactivated during the life of the man you call Podastamu."

"How did you not know this already?" Padalmo said.

"We have not returned to your world in several thousand years, Padalmo. We only did so now because it was in route to another destination, and your gate had been deactivated. We wished to solve a mystery."

Moses and Anders shared a look. Anders nodded, and spoke. Moses translated.

"That and we seeded this planet so it could produce a set of resources we find valuable. Stable super-heavy elements. In fact, your people were contracted to produce it. Podastamu was no prophet of ours. He was a man, probably with his own intents and desires. Perhaps even a liar."

Padalmo leaned back in the chair. The revelations were not faith-shaking, at least, not in the way that he had expected when Moses warned them. It was more a realization of how the mundane can be built up to the spiritual. He had performed everything according to faith, and had been rewarded with the truth, a truth that seemed far more fantastical, and yet less magical, than he had anticipated. The memories of the desert came back to him.

"I had no faith," he said, looking up at Moses. "I had no faith in you, or God. I had planned to fake my way through the trial of the prophet to gain a comfortable life. I planned on being a liar."

"And now you will be tasked with telling the truth," Moses said, translating for Anders. "Just because you lack faith does not mean that God did not have a hand in bringing you to us. We have need of you."

Padalmo nodded.

DAVID VAN DYKE STEWART

*

Malcolm Macbeth stood behind Claribel at her office terminal, which he noted was both neater and messier than his own, crowded with mementos and pictures but free of empty coffee cups and other refuse that Malcolm made himself clean up only when he was bored. Claribel leaned back in her chair as she cued up the video. A middle-aged man appeared. He looked dirty and disheveled, with a short grey beard that began below his eyes and terminated below a high, grey collar.

"This Richard McManigan," the man said softly. His voice creaked, as if he had not used it in a long time. "This will be my final log and statement, and the final personnel log of Quantum Gate One-Three-Six, serving Terranostra and the outer core worlds." He took a breath and looked down.

"Turn it up," Malcolm said. Claribel complied, and the hiss of fans and the man's labored breathing became audible.

"From what we have seen on our planet, and heard over coms, I must assume that nobody living will view this message. For the past month, we have attempted to send word to the outer core worlds of the situation planetside, in hopes one of the clans would put the governments below to task and restore order. Alas, the gate has been malfunctioning. We did our best to restore it, but we found out, all too late, that we have been the victims of sabotage.

PROPHET OF THE GODSEED

"One of our junior technicians by the name of Jeffrey Da'Nil, a man from Panwarke – as if that matters now – had apparently brought the gate down, and thwarted our continued attempts to re-establish contact. We caught him two days ago destroying a data control conduit and a fight ensued. He stabbed another junior technician by the name of Jan Tock. She succumbed to her wounds yesterday. We managed during the altercation to subdue Da'Nil and have him heavily sedated in the infirmary.

"The rest of the crew and I have made the decision to jettison Da'Nil from the airlock, in part as an execution for the crime of murder, having no ability to give trial on the station, and the crime having no shortage of witnesses. However, as a matter of honesty I must also note that the crew and I have entered a survival situation. Our oxygen farm has been poisoned; the plants are all dead. We are running out of O^2, and there is little hope for relief from Terranostra. Removing Da'Nil from the station will increase the time we may continue living for an extra day or two.

"Everybody else is confident we will bring the gate back online in time to be saved, but I am doubtful. The havoc caused by Da'Nil will take weeks to repair as a very hopeful estimate, and we have scant days left of life, and even less of normal cognitive functioning. I have accepted this fate. There is no home to go back to anyway. We watched our world burn." The man shook his head. "Something nobody should ever be subjected to.

"We watched our cities light up with fusion bombs. Green countryside was in flames. Then it all went grey and black. Terranostra is clouded over and will be entering a nuclear winter. I doubt anyone below will survive.

"So this message might be the final testament of the people of Terranostra. I will be encoding within this message some of the data we had time to gather, and some photographs of the carnage, in case anyone returns to this tomb. You will know what happened, though doubtless I will have been long dead by the time you arrive."

The man on the screen took another deep breath. "I have saved away some oxygen from a space suit. Once the rest of the crew begins to lose consciousness, I will tend to their bodies. Besides De'Nil, they have been the finest I have overseen. They deserve your respect for their skill and courage under such pressure. Once I have seen to their burial in space, I will let myself out of the airlock. As captain, it is my duty, and as the last speaker for Terranostra, I must act honorably.

"Please, if you find this, remember who we were. Probe our cultural databanks. It is a shadow of the diversity of our planet, but I hope it will be informative. Do not let this happen elsewhere. Terranostra, signing out."

The screen went blank. Claribel and Malcolm let a solemn and silent minute of space fill them.

PROPHET OF THE GODSEED

"So a nuclear holocaust is what wiped everyone out," Malcolm said. "A fate I am glad is not so typical."

"It must have been very frightening to be up in the gate station all alone, and watching your home be destroyed in silence."

Malcolm nodded. "That thought will haunt me. I think we should keep this video from the others, if we can."

"I agree," Claribel said.

"I'm going to pull Tully off the station," Macbeth said. "If a trained senior tech thinks repairs would take weeks there's no way Tully could manage it, even as good as she is."

"What if we still need to make a jump after all this?" Claribel said.

"Then we'll have to lose the weeks to repair the station," Malcolm said. "But I still intend to find that fuel. It wasn't all consumed in the war, I am certain."

"Why so certain? They could have used it in their weapons."

"Perhaps, but more than half the planet wasn't part of this Panwarke faction. I'm willing to bet that there is still a stockpile, buried down there somewhere."

"What about the planet itself?" Claribel said. "I see history repeating, as our planetsider said."

"You think we should intervene?"

"Yes, frankly. If we can put a stop to this conflict, we could save many millions – and a unique culture. We have the power."

"There are two cultures down there. Which one should we value more? Do we have the right to end one? Do we have the responsibility to save the other?" Macbeth scratched his chin. "I'm not rejecting the idea of intervention, Claribel, just trying to instill some caution."

"I'll work on some potential plans," Claribel said.

"Fair enough," Malcolm said, "but I'm going to be requisitioning some of your department for gravitational surveys."

"I won't need them, but I will need Anders's department, Moses and the planetsider."

"Alright then, let's get to work."

*

Imad hung back as his father dismissed his the military leadership, including, he noted, two high ranking air officers from Pana'Gill, most likely sent by Fadasta ahead of Imalmo's impending announcement. As his father walked through the narrow corridor, Imad put out his hand to catch his attention. With a quick movement, Imalmo moved to the side with his son, pulling him down another dim hallway to a viewing room beyond.

They entered a bright, sunlit room incased in glass, though the ventilation system cooled it well. Just below them was a row of trees by the waterside, their fronds turned toward the sun. A few women reclined on tables underneath the trees, met by servants in flowing robes who hurried between the tables and the entrance to an underground kitchen disguised by shrubberies.

Imalmo watched them, his eyes flicking up toward transports that zoomed overhead.

"The war is hot, but the women are still served cool drinks and fresh bread as if their men are home," Imalmo said.

Imad found himself put off balance by his father's remarks. He knew he had lost the advantage to speak first, but he knew also that it was his father's way to speak calmly and always to acknowledge the moment, and always to adhere to the tradition of how one speaks with an elder. You spoke of the moment, of philosophy, and of God before you spoke to your own passions.

"That is part of why the men fight," Imad said.

"Don't project," Imalmo said. "Who knows the why that lies in each man's heart? It is better to deal with what can be seen. Action and consequence are the realms of nobility, my son. Leave the projection to the artists and the poets."

Imad nodded. He felt suddenly to be at a greater disadvantage. He felt in his head a sudden rebuttal to his father, which would serve as the recusal he needed in this moment, but his father would reject him if he did not follow the old cleric's tradition.

Imad took a breath and said, "Artists and poets are like ink. Good ink draws in crisp lines, but poor ink runs. A good poet will have no need of projection, for he will record things as they truly are. A bad one records a vague shape of what was."

Imalmo nodded. "But also like ink the poets are not what is; they are merely recollections of what is. The man writes his thoughts upon the paper, and so they are recorded, but it was the man that existed and the words are merely a remembrance of that moment before, like all men, he is swept away with change and dies to this world. And who can really say what was in the man's mind when he wrote the words? Yes, Poets are like ink, but it is the man of action who inspires the poet, just as the scribe creates the words on the page."

Imad watched the women laughing. "I wonder if God values their laughter as I value it."

Imalmo chuckled. "I wonder too, but god created women, and he created laughter, so it must have value."

"So you do not know the mind of God," Imad said. In the cool room, he felt sweat burst around his ears, and a bead run down his neck. He had made the gamble.

"You are a clever man," Imalmo said.

"Raised by a clever man," Imad said. "But that was not answering my question."

Imalmo's eyes remained on the scene below. "Not even a prophet knows more than what God chooses him to know."

"Do you know the outcome of this war?"

"I know what will happen if we are not united, yes."

PROPHET OF THE GODSEED

"What about when they find you are not the prophet?"

"I am the prophet." Imalmo turned and regarded his son. "I have been acknowledged prophet by four of the five highlords."

"Is that what makes a prophet?"

"In legal terms, yes."

Imad gritted his teeth. "What about in doctrinal terms?"

"It is said in the Cha'tear that the chosen leaders will then choose a leader to be prophet," Imalmo said. "Most of the prophets were such, and you know it."

"But not for many generations. Without Pana'Tull and Gralfama, there can be no real vote."

"Merely a convenient interpretation to fit our recent problems. I have a majority; that is all which matters."

"And what of Jafta?"

"Jafta will join, or do what it has always done and stand apart. It doesn't matter what Jafta does; what matters is that we have the others and the others will not perish." Imalmo held up his hand. "My son, I appreciate your thoughts on faith and on the future. I will heed what you have said, but trust me when I say that God is guiding me to preserve our people, forever. The time is drawing close, closer than you think, when the darksider threat will be eliminated forever."

"How close?"

"Close. For now, let us watch the laughter, for there may be little in the days to come."

Imad sighed. He did as his father bid, and watched the milling of the people on the shore.

"I have a task for you, Imad," Imalmo said at length. "A most important task, to you and to me."

"Yes?"

"Requisition a transport and a good pilot. Take your mother, Fala, and all their younger children to the country estate."

"What?"

"I anticipate a swift and bloody battle with the outsiders. Pana'Chu may fall."

"But why not your entire household?"

"If you wish to preserve at least a portion of what you have, best to divide it. Nowhere is truly safe, but part of my family here, in citadel, and part in the countryside where the darkside warriors will not be looking for the wives and sons of the Highlord, is the best option to secure the continuance of our line. If we fall here, you shall be Highlord."

"I understand," Imad said.

"Take a last look, then be quick about it."

Imad nodded, and watched the women on the shore for a final time.

*

"What are we looking at?" Anders said. He reclined in a high-backed chair in a conference room packed with terminals. A large central display showed a satellite image of unknown land. Beside him Padalmo, looking uncomfortable in the articulating work chairs, tried to discern what the image was.

PROPHET OF THE GODSEED

"This represents a column of people and equipment that I believe constitutes a fighting force," Claribel said. She cued through a few more images. "Here and here, we see the same sort of movement, converging on this metropolitan area."

Padalmo sat forward and spoke quickly to Moses.

"That's his city," Moses said. "Pana'Chu."

Claribel nodded. "It's not the only one." She showed two more metropolitan areas, with similar pictures of columns of equipment moving through mountain passes. "The faction that controls the Western side of the habitable zone, as well as all settlements on the dark side, is making a concerted effort to converge on all other metropolitan areas."

"A blitzkrieg, of sorts," Anders said. "Surely the other faction has defenses in place."

"Rudimentary, yes," Claribel said. "For the most part I have found that fighting occurs primarily in zones that are constantly conflicted." She put up an image of a dry countryside, rocky and bearing little in the way of greenery. Padalmo spoke, his voice sad, but calm.

"He says that area was once a city, but was destroyed a long time ago," Moses said. Padalmo spoke again, hurriedly. "He says the time of renewal is nearing. The fire will return."

"Interesting," Claribel said. "A few millennia ago, the population was decimated by a nuclear war and ensuing winter. Perhaps he hints at such a return? If so-"

Claribel was interrupted by the door opening, ushering in a young woman with a shock of red hair about her shoulders. She carried a heavy bag and a large cup in one hand.

"Sorry I'm late Aunt Claire, just needed some coffee."

"Glad to have you, Tully," Claribel said. "I should remind you to use ship rank when addressing others at work, not family relation."

"What did I miss?" Tully said, swinging around a chair beside Moses and ignoring Claribel's statement. Moses glanced at her then consciously looked away.

"Just some nuclear war," Anders said. Tully frowned at him. "You know, I'm wondering which faction has the nuclear threat."

"Probably the darksiders," Moses said. "They are more technically advanced."

"Why not both sides?" Tully said.

"Because the threat of mutually assured destruction usually keeps each faction from letting loose on each other," Anders said.

"Yes, but aren't they religious zealots?" Tully said. She looked at Claribel. "I read the brief on the way in from the gate."

"Padalmo just talked about fire and rebirth," Claribel said.

"He said similar things to the chieftain," Anders said. "So at least his faction might have some religious belief that allows for its own population to be destroyed."

PROPHET OF THE GODSEED

"I think you are wrong," Moses said. "The faithful faction is devoted to opposing technological singularity, not self-destruction."

"You're getting too close to the planetsider," Anders said. "You're seeing things from his view and adding your own prejudice. Don't let your own experience in the Earth collective cloud your vision. The western faction has *not* achieved singularity. The eastern faction has specific mythology concerning the death of the world, and rebirth. These are the facts."

Moses shook his head. "I still think you are wrong."

"Listen to Anders, Moses," Tully said. "I know you've made a new friend, but you need to think of this objectively." Moses fell silent and turned back to the screen.

"Suppose this blitzkrieg is designed to capture the nuclear arsenal," Anders said. "That would effectively remove the nuclear threat. Possibly end the war."

"By allowing them to conquer without fear of massive retaliation," Moses said.

"Why wouldn't the other faction do the same, to the darksiders?" Claribel said.

"It's something I've been mulling in my head for a while, since we first talked to Padalmo," Anders said. "How the population has adapted to near constant warfare. Padalmo's culture does it by embracing polygamy, which allows for population growth despite massive losses in the male population. The other faction has to have some kind of similar adaptation, but it appears they have plenty of personnel and equipment."

"We haven't witnessed the way they wage war," Tully said. "Maybe our planetsider's faction has been really losing this whole time, and the ones he calls darksiders have been incredibly efficient at combat. So efficient that the constant war has had little or no impact on their ability to grow their population and their army. Maybe their equipment is highly durable as well."

Claribel spoke up. "They've been thinking very long term, then. They would have continued the conflict, drawing the enemy in and exhausting his resources, while secretly increasing their own. Then they can execute this Blitzkrieg and remove the nuclear threat once and for all."

"So what do we do?" Anders said. "It seems like they might be solving their own problem."

"It's very uncertain," Claribel said. "First, we need to quickly gather some data to see if this blitz hypothesis actually has some truth to it. We have to consider the risks of nuclear war in the event of the aggressive faction's failure, and what might happen if they are successful."

"Singularity is still a fear, then," Tully said.

"That is my fear," Moses said. He looked to Anders. "My apologies for taking sides. The fact that my remaining implants can interface with their network so fluidly should still frighten all of you. I know what it is like to be inside a singularity."

PROPHET OF THE GODSEED

"Alright, I think we have a framework for the next few hours of work," Claribel said. "Anders, I want your department to analyze the nuclear capabilities of Padalmo's faction, and to evaluate chances of neutralization on the part of that faction's enemies. Moses, I want you to assist Tully in the development of some measures to halt that faction's progress toward singularity. I have requisitioned a crew to work under you. They should already be in terminal room four. I'll be rotating as director." She nodded. "Get to it."

Tully took a sip of her coffee and stood up. "Looks like you're with me, kiddo."

"Kiddo?" Moses said, standing up. Tully winked at him and turned toward the door. Moses looked questioningly at Anders, who smirked.

"Try to stay on task, my friend," Anders said.

Moses rubbed his head, confused. "Wait, captain!" he said to Claribel as she reached the door. "What do we do with Padalmo?"

Claribel smiled at him. "He's clearly become your charge. You decide." With that, she stepped out the door, leaving Moses puzzled.

Bread Upon the Water

16 months earlier, ship time

STARS FILLED Malcom Macbeth's vision, bright colors shifting and blurring: artifacts of the divergent passage of time as they cruised near the speed of light. He wasn't just watching space go by; he was watching time go by, the galaxy beyond the ship hurtling forward in normal time while things onboard passed infinitely slow by comparison. His eyes fixed on one star to the left of the ship, a supergiant with far too much cosmic radiation to risk a close approach. It had been slowly shifting from blue to white as they ceased to close with it, and Malcolm knew it would shift to red once the fleet-ship moved away from it in earnest.

He stood alone on the bare walkway, surrounded by superstructure and windows layered with carbon and corundum that separated him from the vacuum of space. It was one of the few places on the ship he could count on being deserted, and he could never quite understand why; the stars were beautiful, the view astoundingly wide, if a bit sickening to look down upon. He breathed deeply, trying to dispel what was left of the anxiety that rushed in when he had received his daughter's communique.

Not so long ago you were young, he thought as he pictured his daughter on her wedding day. *When next we meet, you will be old, like me. Whatever will I do with you?* Plans were already working their way into twisted paths in his mind, drawing him away from the jitter of reunions and to the hard work of managing the massive enterprise that was Clan Macbeth, spread over many worlds and controlling capital that would be unfathomable to a planetsider. *I've needed a new XO. And with Anders...* he smiled.

"Sir?" The voice of Tully over the com echoed in the dark chamber.

"What is it?"

"A transmission."

"What type?"

"High-energy UHF. Sort of. Signal degradation indicates a distant signal. Or..."

"Or what?"

"Or it indicates a closer signal with a failing repeater."

"What about triangulation?" Macbeth scratched his beard.

"There's just the one burst. A few months back Galactic standard. Just came in."

"What else about it?"

"I'm still analyzing, but it appears to be a 256 bit binary message."

"Binary, eh? Is it what I think it is?"

PROPHET OF THE GODSEED

"Might be, given the protocol. We're working on the language codec. Should only take a few minutes more."

Macbeth walked over to a nearby terminal, and it leapt to life, illuminating his face from below. "Give me a moment and I will cue up some coding tables that should match." His fingers flitted over the screen and a few files dropped over into Tully's queue.

"Earth codecs?"

"You'll note our course and distance. It's a possibility. And given that it's a binary signal... Well, just see. I have a feeling."

A few seconds passed, and then Tully replied. "There we go. It's just a bunch of math equations, so probably just a data package. Could it really be an Earth message? I thought they stopped sending them thousands of years ago."

"They did, but there were also ships and probes from sent out from Earth."

"That's quite a leap," Tully said.

"It is. Just a guess."

"From before the singularity?"

"Perhaps after. I've heard rumors."

"Rumors, guesses, and feelings. That's not like you, grandpa."

Malcolm smiled, knowing Tully could not see him. "True."

"Second ping just came in. One month in standard time after the first."

"Can you triangulate?"

"Murray!" Tully shouted before the com released her voice. "Yes, sir. It's almost dead ahead, a few arcseconds to port, as we're heading. A little less than a light-year away."

Malcolm rapped his knuckles on a nearby handrail. "Just equations? No words?"

"Near as we can tell. Complex equations, but I'm not finding any pattern that I would call linguistic."

"What about vectors?"

"I have no idea, sir."

"Anders will be on deck shortly," Malcolm said, knowing his son would arrive precisely at the end of his father's shift, nearly to the second. Something had been consuming the young man, but Malcolm could not yet discern what. "Have him take a look at it. The nature of the equation might be an attempt at communication, rather than just a packet of data. It's a curiosity he would love to solve."

"If you say so."

"I do. I'll be up in the bridge in a minute. Macbeth out."

He killed the com and spent another few seconds looking out at the stars.

*

Anders stepped onto the bridge. He noticed the empty captain's console and chair (though he knew his father rarely sat when he was running the ship) and looked around briefly. He noticed the patriarch leaning over the chair at Tully's messy station, his eyes flitting over a green-lit display.

PROPHET OF THE GODSEED

"Sir."

Malcolm turned and raised an eyebrow to Anders. "On time, as usual."

Anders nodded, then relaxed. "What's the dig, sir?"

"Couple of data pulses over the last few hours," Tully answered. She nodded to Macbeth without taking her eyes off the screen. "Gramps thinks it might be from Earth. Maybe even a ship. *I* think it's a beacon or a probe."

"What's the nature of the data?" Anders said.

"Take a look," Macbeth said, and then strode over to his command station. He opened up several display panels and looked through them. With the touch of a button, the tablet at Anders's belt lit up. Anders looked and scrolled quickly through a few screens.

"Interesting. I can tell you right now it's not a data packet meant for a particular recipient."

"What makes you think that?" Tully asked.

"Coherent and self-contained. This is 256 bit binary?"

"You bet. Ones and zeroes, just like in the bible," Tully said.

Malcolm chuckled. "Clearly I have failed the clan as theologian. Anders, you said it was coherent?"

"Yes. Well, I should say that I believe that it is coherent. These aren't pieces of random data, they are complete abstract equations. Some are geometric and four dimensional."

"Take a look while you have the bridge, will you?" Macbeth stepped away from the command station and nodded at Anders.

"Not much else to do, eh?" Anders said.

"Let's hope. I'm heading up to get some sleep. Try not to wake me unless it's urgent."

"Yes sir."

Malcolm turned and walked toward the lift. He paused as the door opened for him and looked off to the side, his brow wrinkled.

"Sir?"

"If you determine it's actually from Earth."

"Yes?"

"Collect what data you can. Then it is probably best to destroy it."

"What if it's not just a probe?"

"Orders stand."

*

"It's moved another point-ten of an arc second into our path, judging by the last pulse," Tully said.

"Fortuitous. Intercept?" Anders leaned over his displays, each showing a realization of the four dimensional geometric equations they had gathered from the data pulses.

"We'll miss it by about 500 billion kilometers. It's also going to traverse our course about 20 billion k positive Z."

"That's not a terribly large course correction."

"Not terribly, no," Tully said. "But you know the old man."

"How much time would we lose if we decelerated and shifted trajectory to at least get a good sensor sweep?"

"Let me see," Tully said. She flipped over to a new screen on her display. "Two years."

Anders tilted his head. "That's pretty reasonable. We'd still be well within the window we presented at Edi."

"Are you ordering a correction, Andy?"

"Sir."

"It's madam." Tully shot her uncle a smile. Anders raised an eyebrow. "Should we wake the old man?"

"Probably not worth his time," Anders said. "We make two year corrections all the time. Besides, he left me in charge of this situation. I'll go ahead and enter our course. We'll at least be able to do a sensor sweep and destroy the probe if needed."

"Aye." Tully looked across the flat workspace of her station at Vanessa, who nodded back, then set to calculating the risks and obstacles of the new course.

*

The ship lurched slightly as acceleration began again on the new heading. The anti-inertial gravity field switched orientations, stirring up a slight queasy feeling that Anders had never found palatable, despite having grown up on the ship. He watched the coffee in Tully's cup float up, attempting to make a sphere at the slight loss, then slosh down below the rim. She took a quick sip and looked up at the main viewer, upon which Anders had projected the data relative to the probe. Jon, the sensor manager and back-up helmsman, turned around and pulled his chair up beside her.

"That stuff smells like death," he said, peering at the top of her black cup.

"One of the ways you know it'll work as promised," she replied, cracking a smile but not bothering to look away from the screen and meet Jon's eyes.

Vanessa, her hands flitting over her keys, said, "Coffee doesn't have to taste bad to be effective. I have a cache of beans from the last port, if you're looking for a roast that's actually palatable. Some of us actually have a sense of taste."

Tully forced out a false chuckle that ended up sounding like something between a cough and choke.

"Bah, gimme tea," Jon said. He took a drought out of his own tall cup.

"Now, there's two equations – three, actually, that stand out among the rabble of data," Anders said. He highlighted and expanded several sections.

"What makes them stand out?" Tully said. "Just looks like a standard proof series."

"They are proofs, for the most part," Anders said. "Except these number sequences are all based on prime numbers. They are designed to not look like noise."

"Except they do look like noise."

"Only to your average human brain," Anders said.

Tully shot a shocked look at Jon. "Did you hear that? He just called me average."

"He said your brain was average," Jon said.

PROPHET OF THE GODSEED

"So you don't care about my mind," Tully said. "Typical man." She turned away from Jon, who rubbed his cheek bashfully with the palm of his hand. He could not see what Anders did, which was a smirk cracking her freckled face. Vanessa frowned at her, but Tully pretended not to notice.

"Turn away all attention, Tully, and you're going to find that nobody-"

Anders cleared his throat. "The number sequence and these equations are designed, or should I say I believe they were designed, to communicate design itself."

"What?" Jon said. He continued rubbing his cheek.

"They are un-random, which, by definition, means they were designed. Designed to be un-random – to look designed."

"Sounds like an existential question," Tully said. "All that talk about design."

"The concept of design is what makes them stand out in a noisy environment," Anders went on.

"What noise?" Jon said. "Background radiation? EM radiation from stars and dwarfs? Binary is a hell of a long way from that."

"It is," Anders said.

"Maybe the creators of the probe wanted to make sure it could be understood by someone who wasn't specifically looking for it." Tully leaned forward and cued up a number series on the screen. "Binary is the simplest language that I can think of. If we look at this area here, we see that each of these numbers is surrounded by a field of on/off messages across the broadcast spectrum. A bunch of ones and zeros. An alien intelligence could easily understand those data pulses to be on-off sequences. Then they could decode the number sequence after that."

"Yeah, but to what end? A bunch of numbers. So what?" Jon said. "The binary is enough to communicate intelligence, right? There must be an actual message in there that we don't understand."

"Definitely," Anders said. He cued up the original sequence. "But not this sequence. It's purely mathematical." He smiled and leaned back in his chair, looking out at the stars. "I think the old man is right."

"Earth?" Tully said.

Anders nodded. "I think about the beings that might have created these transmissions. It's not enough to broadcast in binary. You have to broadcast math as well, to prove that what you are sending out isn't just part of a random data packet, because Earth now – or when this probe was created – was in a very literal sense nothing but a sea of massive data packets. When things are encoded or encrypted, only a piece of them makes sense. They designed this probe to make its data stand out to anyone listening or sniffing up transmissions, partly by being self-contained. The beings made a common enough assumption – that the macro is the same as the micro. That worlds outside of Earth would be as noisy as Earth is."

"And that they would also be singularized," Jon said.

Anders nodded.

"Interesting hypothesis," Tully said. "Can we test it?"

"Once we get closer to the probe, I imagine that shall be automatic," Anders said.

*

"Sensors are aligned for a sweep," Vanessa said. "I can drop our own sensor burst probe now. We should be able to map the dorsal side of the probe, and then pick up our readings a few million miles on the other side of it."

Anders scratched his chin. "That doesn't give us the options the old man wanted."

"Of destroying it?" Vanessa said. "I can drop an armed probe capable of that, if you wish."

"He's looking for an excuse to drop speed and sweep in real time," Tully said.

"Maybe," Anders said. "If we speed on past it we can choose to destroy it or not, but we cannot choose to recover it."

"You heard what the old man said," Tully said. "It's from Earth, yeah? We should count on needing to destroy it."

"We only suspect at the moment," Anders said. "There are always other possibilities. Run our time loss, if you will. Jon, prep our reverse engines."

"Yes sir," Jon said.

Tully sighed and then proceeded to get to work. Anders stood at the front of the bridge, looking out at the stars, and narrowed his eyes. He felt the decelerators kick it, pushing against the ship's near light-speed inertial velocity. The gravitational fields that held that inertial play at bay swirled around them, and cups shook on the surfaces of the tables.

"It's close," Vanessa said. "About 500k kilometers."

"Hit it with a frequency burst."

"Aye." A few seconds went by. "Returned. It's larger than we thought. About a kilometer long."

"Hell of a probe," Jon said.

"Looks like we wouldn't have been able to destroy it with an armed sensor probe anyway," Anders said.

Vanessa went on as Anders took in the data on his own screen at the front of the railed walk that hemmed in the bridge section. "The hull is a titanium-steel alloy. There is significant oxidation, and integrity is weak. The interior appears to be pressurized."

"So clearly not a probe," Tully said.

"Energy signatures are fluctuating. Engines appear to be non-functional, or at least totally powered down. They're running on inertia alone. I'll try to penetrate the interior on higher-energy bands."

"No," Anders said. "Wait. I don't want to ionize the interior if there is life inside."

"We're not close enough to use infrared."

Anders looked at Tully and Jon. "You heard her. Bring us in."

"Aye. I'm powering up defense systems as well."

"Sir? Maybe we should bring in one wing instead of the whole fleet-ship," Vanessa said.

PROPHET OF THE GODSEED

Anders nodded and thought to himself. "Goldwing, then. Randall is usually up about now."

"I'll wake the old man," Tully said.

Anders stared at her for a few seconds then said, "He'll be awake by the time we get there for sure."

*

Randall pushed the engines hard, and Anders had to grip a handrail to stay upright before Goldwing's systems could compensate for the sudden change of acceleration. Anders looked out a nearby window to the rest of the fleet-ship, a mass of angled metal that contained the whole of the spacefaring clan amid its dozen sections. He took a deep breath as Icarus shrank to insignificance and disappeared.

"That looks like her," Tully said. She pulled up magnified image of a ship, cast in a hue of colors accelerate from infrared to the visible spectrum. It was an elongated tube flattened on one side, with two engine arrays at either end that were as dark as the rest of the ship.

"Definitely a ship," Randall said. He scratched his beard and made a slight course correction. "It's cold."

"Somewhere around 100 degrees Kelvin," Tully said.

"Has to be warmer than that," Randall said. "Its systems were active and sending out data."

Anders leaned over and looked closer at the projection. "Whatever part of that ship that was running communications may only be powering up for the data transmission, then going back into a low-power mode."

Randall pursed his lips. "Doesn't look like there are any windows."

Anders nodded. "That would be consistent with what we know if this ship were sent from Earth post-collectivization. There are no reasons to have a human drone appreciate the view when external sensors and the internal computer can make all the navigation decisions."

"Maybe that's why we're not seeing the com array," Randall said.

"We'd see some lingering heat, I imagine," Tully said.

"Even after all this time?"

"No medium for the kinetic energy to radiate," Tully said. "That and there has to be a power source in there somewhere."

"What about life signs?" Anders said.

"On an ice cube?" Randall said.

"Stasis," Anders said. "And this is definitely a ship."

"Let me see if I can find any heat signatures below the hull," Tully said. The spectrum of the image shifted and displayed an almost black shape, outlined in hues of midnight blue. A pale blue dominated one spot of the ship. Tully pointed at it. "I think that's the power plant. Still pretty cold. Maybe they're running on battery."

"Like I said, an ice cube," Randall said.

PROPHET OF THE GODSEED

"Let me play with it a bit," Tully said. "If there's something to be found in there I *will* find it."

"Let's see about data extraction," Anders said." I presume there is no access point that is broadcasting." He lit up a nearby terminal and started working through a few routines. "I'll see if I can energize a physical terminal, pop it to life."

"Janet's pretty good at that," Randall said. "I could wake her."

"I think I have it," Anders said. "Communications is my specialty."

"Not for long, I hear," Randall said. "Word is the big guy is pushing you up to executive officer."

Anders smiled. "Just rumors."

"Anders? Report." It was Macbeth. A nearby screen lit up with the old man's face. He was frowning.

"Tully's working on life signs. I'm attempting to create a virtual uplink and hopefully extract some data."

"Where is it from?"

Anders paused a moment, intent on his screen. "Not sure just yet."

"Like hell you aren't," Macbeth said. His signature popped up on Anders's terminal screen.

"This data could be invaluable. We haven't dared to examine Earth in millennia."

"When you get it, I want it put into physical isolation, not just virtual isolation. Don't attempt to run any software you extract outside of a totally secure and isolated environment."

"Understood, sir. I wouldn't risk it." Anders smiled. "I think I found a terminal." He powered up his array and energized the rear of the ship. The hull on Tully's screen flashed yellow and green as the ice on the outside of the ship vaporized with ionization. Anders's screen flashed with a flurry of binary.

"Hey!" Tully said. "I was practically seeing inside."

"Sorry kiddo," Anders said. "Damn it!" The stream of data stopped.

"You burned out the terminal," Macbeth said.

"No!" Anders said. "No, that's not it. Something else happened. Some sort of manual security device. The terminal is still functioning. It's just not responding anymore."

"Other systems on the ship might be leaching the power," Tully said. "I see a few places heating up. Electrical and thermal activity, too."

"It might be time to cut our losses and destroy it," the clan chief said.

"It's definitely disabled," Randall said. "I can make double sure though. A couple of quick graviton waves will crush her engines and keep her afloat permanently."

"What about weapon systems?" Macbeth said.

"No trace," Tully said. "Whatever she was built for, the makers didn't consider combat at all. That hull is nearly seamless besides a few doors. No weapons ports to be found."

"We could go in," Anders said. "Take a look. Maybe extract the databanks manually."

"Out of the question," Macbeth said. "If you can't access its drives remotely, destroy the craft and move to rejoin the ship."

"Understood."

"Good." Macbeth turned and looked to another screen for a moment. "I'm going to re-accelerate Icarus back to within a few micro deviations of maximum. I'm transmitting the trajectory and acceleration information to your computer. When you finish tidying up, rejoin. Communications will be severely offset, so you'll be on your own. I don't want to lose another year out here poking at dead spacecraft. Macbeth out."

The com screen went dark. Anders looked over to Tully, who seemed oblivious to the exchange.

"I guess that sinks that idea," Randall said. "Too bad. This ice cube has me curious."

"Me too," Anders said. "Let me try a little higher burst. Can you get us in a bit closer? Maybe within normal visual range?"

"Visual range? Like out the window visual range?" Randall said.

"Well, a few k is probably close enough."

"Dangerous with an Earth ship. Besides, the old man said-"

"He said not to board it," Anders said. "But I want a look at this thing."

Randall shrugged and pushed Goldwing into motion again. Tully spilled coffee on her hand and cursed.

"She's jumpy," Anders said.

"I am not," Tully said.

"I meant the ship."

"It's the new thruster mods," Randall said. "Better than what we had, but now the inertial systems can't quite keep up."

"And so the cycle continues. Aha!" Anders brought up on the main viewer an image of an elongated double-engine ship. He toyed with a few settings and the image got brighter, revealing a long, metallic fuselage painted with a series of letters that glowed dimly in the amplified light of the nearest red dwarf. They formed incomprehensible words.

"What's it say?" Randall said.

"It's just a serial identifier, I think," Anders said. "But those are definitely Latin letters."

"So it really is from Earth."

"It's definitely human. Could be from one of the dead worlds, but yes, I do think it is from Earth." Anders punched up his terminal. "I'm going to try again to access the computer remotely." Another screen full of data bits flashed by, then stopped.

"Hold up!" Tully said. "You've flashed a power plant back to life, or something. I'm detecting a lot of electrical systems, and the ship's heating up."

"What kind of systems?" Anders said.

"How would I know? I don't know anything about Earth ships."

"Quick," Anders said, "Let's disable it." He shuffled over to another station while Randall began to pivot Goldwing slightly.

"We're in mass altering range."

Anders nodded. "I at least know what engines look like. Let's crush 'em."

A loud hum filled the cabin as the ship began to vibrate. The conical engine outlets on each side of the ship crumpled. Sparks flashed white-hot on the main viewer.

"She's dead," Randall said.

"Systems are cutting out," Tully said. "Looks like you killed the main power plant."

"Shit," Anders said. "So much for the drives."

"Too bad about what grandpa said," Tully added. "Wait." She leaned forward and pulled her hands apart, magnifying the infrared image of the dead ship. "There's some afterglow. Here." She pointed at a few splotches standing out through the metal hull of the ship.

Randall leaned over and squinted. "What do you think those are?"

"Maybe the computers are still radiating heat," Tully said.

"Check for life signs," Anders said. "Full scan. We're in range for the works."

"Aye aye," Tully said. She looked at Randall and said, "So much for an ice cube, eh?"

"We don't know that yet," Randall said. "It'll take you a few minutes. I'm going to hit the head." The helmsman stood up and exited the small bridge.

Anders stood over Tully's shoulder and watched a stream of data build up in several windows. "What about CO_2?" he said.

"No windows to do a spectral analysis."

"What about trying to measure internal cabin pressure?"

Tully nodded. "It's definitely pressurized."

"What about changes?"

"You going to do this job, or am I?" Tully said.

"Sorry," Anders said. "I just had a thought. The ship was very cold. Cold enough to cause carbon dioxide to solidify."

"Ah, and the dry ice should be evaporating." Tully pulled up a new window on her display. "Looks like there's some increasing stress on the hull. Very subtle. Whatever is in there, it once was breathing, and the CO_2 traps have failed. Definitely not a probe. Hmn..." Tully trailed off and pulled a thermal image of the cabin back up.

"What is it?"

"Heat is dissipating in several parts of the ship, sinking out with some venting from the engine, but not here. See?" She pointed to two faint splotches midway through the other ship.

"Body heat," Anders said. "Has to be." He turned to his own displays. "Power plants are offline."

"What do we do?" Tully said. "They'll either asphyxiate or freeze without the power to run whatever stasis machinery they are using, or to run the gas traps."

Anders rested his chin on his fist, and shifted on his feet. He sighed.

"We better prep a transport, and fix up some EV suits."

Tully stopped and looked at him. "You heard the old man."

"I did. But those are people in there. Human beings."

"Hardly," Tully said. "They're drones of the Earth singularity. You know they don't even have thought, right?"

"We don't know that," Anders said. "None of the clans have actually captured an Earth human... ever that I know of."

"You mean none of them have been stupid enough to," Tully said. "They're like walking hack boxes."

"That's beyond exaggeration. Separated from the network they're probably helpless. And this computer is dead."

"You don't know that."

"Suit up, Tully."

She turned and frowned at him as Randall came back in, buttoning his jacket. "What did I miss?"

Tully smirked and nodded toward Randall. "Is he on the boarding party?"

"No, I need someone at the helm here. Anyone else you could wake up?"

"Willem."

"Have him meet us in the transport bay."

"I'll have him head up here," Randall said. "I'm not going to let some planetsider take my chance to see inside an earth ship."

Tully chuckled. "Ten minutes ago you were calling it a boring hunk of ice."

"Ten minutes ago it was." Randall the punched the com and yelled into it, "Willem! Drag your ass out of bed; I need you to watch the com."

"I'm supposed to sleep for another three hours."

"Sorry, but I need you up here."

"I'll tell mom."

"No you won't."

There was a pause, then Willem said, "You owe me."

"Noted." Randall released the com and turned to Anders. "I'll get to work on prepping the transport. Willem will be here in a minute or two. There's EV suits a few doors down, on the left."

CHAPTER 6
Unity and Separation

Malcolm Macbeth walked behind the row of terminals facing the bridge section of *Icarus*, checking over the work of his crew, pulled partly from Claribel's science team and partly from the crew of helmsmen and navigators sitting mostly idle as the fleet-ship hung about Terranostra. The blast doors of the huge, semi-spherical windows were peeled back, flooding the wide, steel-floored room with the light of stars and the corona of sunlight that marked Terranostra's inhabitable zone. Seeing a planet in reality, fleshed out with vivid and living colors always inspired Macbeth to appropriate modes of thinking.

He paused behind the workstation of Jon, one of his helmsmen. He watched the young man quickly orient a series of translucent graphics on top of aerial photos of the habitable zone. For each rectangular section of pale green, he made slight adjustments, bumping the images slightly to the left or right, up or down.

"What are we doing here?" Macbeth said, putting his hands behind his back.

"I retrieved some geographical and topical maps from the data on board the old quantum gate," Jon said, turning back to look at the chieftain. His spectacles rimmed green eyes that were seemingly more rested than the rest of the crew. "I'm looking for persistent features, like mountains, to line the images up properly. The magnetic poles haven't shifted much in the last few millennia, so it should be short work."

"To what end, helmsman?" Macbeth said.

"Gravitational surveys take time ," Jon said. "I thought if we had a better idea of past geography, we could focus our sensor sweeps on the most likely areas to contain stockpiles."

"That's a good idea," Macbeth said. "However, I notice you are ignoring the sunward desert areas and the dark side. That's more than eighty percent of the planet's surface."

"Sir?" Jon's face scrunched up. "Nobody lived there."

"You are thinking outside the box, but still staring at it," Macbeth said. "Our former inhabitants did not necessarily live where they mined heavy elements, nor did they necessarily spend energy bringing them to population centers for stockpiling. Mineral deposits don't care much for where the sun is shining. Expand what you are doing. I want comparative maps for the entire planet, especially the desert side, understand?"

"Yes sir," Jon said.

"As soon as you are done aligning a section of the map, I want you to send it to Timothy's station. Did you hear that?" Macbeth turned over to Timothy, one of the engineers.

"Yes sir," Timothy said, throwing his current screen downward so that it disappeared. He brought up the translucent green readout that Jon was generating.

"Use your best judgment for focused gravimetric scans," Macbeth said. "Delegate the second array to Vanessa. Same instructions for you, ensign."

"Understood, sir." Vanessa's dark hair was tied back, and she focused intently on the screens that Timothy was shuffling over to her.

Macbeth stepped past the workstations, out onto the steel gangplank where helm control sat, with a wide, 180-degree view of space in every direction. He woke up one of the helm terminals and began shuffling through Jon's work. He looked up at the image of planet and activated the massive heads-up display that was integrated into the shielded corundum windows of the bridge. In a few seconds, the planet's outer edges were covered in overlapping sections of translucent green.

"That's better," Macbeth said to himself, smiling. He opened up a com channel to the entire ship. His voice boomed. "*Icarus* will be moving orbitally under thruster conditions in five minutes. Those working in zero-G should return to a gravity stabilized work area. Inertial disruptions should be minimal. Wing detachment requests should be sent to the helm." He dropped his formal tone for a moment. "In case you are wondering, we are moving 'round to the bright side for better visuals. Enjoy the view while we move. Once again, the ship will begin moving in five minutes. Macbeth out."

"Sir?" Jon said, pulling his chair around and standing up.

"What?" Macbeth said. He moved between helm consoles, beginning charging sequences for orbital thrusters.

"Did you... need me, sir?" Jon paused at the end of the causeway.

"I know how to pilot my own ship, Johnny," Macbeth said, and sat down at the center console. "Besides, you know best what you're doing over there. Keep at it. I just feel like I need to see the whole of the desert. Trust me on this."

"Yes, sir," Jon said, and returned to his workstation. "Let me know if she gives you any trouble. I've tweaked analogue controls to me own liking. Maybe they won't suit you."

"I can handle it," Macbeth said, and attended to the orbital navigation displays. He added quietly to himself. "I have a good feeling about this."

*

"I'm going to lose reception."

"What?" Tully turned her attention away from the display to Moses, who sat by idly with Padalmo. The steady chime warning of thruster movement sounded softly in the background.

PROPHET OF THE GODSEED

"If we move to the sunward side of the planet, I'm going to lose my uplink with the dark side's internet," Moses said.

With a flick, Tully tapped into Claribel's com. *Punched* was a better term for it, for rather than the usual digital request, ring tone, and user acceptance of a com link, Tully could open a channel on ship coms that the user had no way to decline.

"Captain, this is Tully," she said quickly. "Moses is concerned we'll lose his implant connections if we go to the bright side of the planet. We should disconnect Grey Wing and continue working while on the dark side."

"Damnit Tully," Claribel said over the com. "You know protocols-"

"No time for that sir," Tully went on. "We're leaving in less than five minutes. It takes 120 seconds to disconnect from the rest of *Icarus*. That means you have about that much time to make a decision."

Claribel sighed audibly over the com. "How important is Moses's uplink to your goals?"

"As important as Greywing's hardware," Tully said. "If I have a hope of disabling or modifying their network from the outside, I need to understand the ins and outs of how it interfaces with remote devices, implants, security... Moses is everything in that capacity."

"Alright, Tully," Claribel said. "I'll put in the request immediately."

"Way ahead of you." Tully *punched* into Macbeth's com. "Chieftain, sir. We need to disconnect Grey

Wing and stay on the dark side to accomplish department goals."

"Do it," Macbeth said.

"Understood," Claribel said, sounding tired and annoyed. "I'll head to the helm."

The com went quiet. Tully looked over to Moses and raised her eyebrows with a slight smile, satisfied with herself.

"That seemed easy," Moses said. He wiped his forehead with his hand. "Macbeth didn't even ask for an explanation."

"The chieftain delegates with trust. He knows I wouldn't ask for something without reason."

"What if you did ask without a reason?" Moses said.

"I wouldn't," Tully said. She took a sip of coffee and turned back to her display. "You look a bit flush. Maybe you should lose the jacket, eh?"

"It's always the same temperature in here. I'm usually comfortable with my jacket on."

"Eh," was all the response Tully gave him before diving back into sheets of data spread across her display. Moses grumbled and removed his jacket.

"I don't think she cares much for you," Padalmo said, startling Moses slightly.

Moses shook his head. "We are friends," he said in Padalmo's language.

"And that's all you'll ever be, if you keep on like that."

PROPHET OF THE GODSEED

"What's the problem with that?" Moses turned to his own terminal and began absent-mindedly looking through sensor analysis of the internet below, which he could not make heads or tails of.

"You tell me," Padalmo said with a smile. "You're blushing so bad when she looks at you your face starts to look like a ja'a fruit."

Moses rubbed his neck. "This is not a physical response I'm familiar with."

Padalmo chuckled. "Well, just so you know, I don't think her lack of affection is fixed in stone. She just doesn't notice you much. Look at her flit away with that machine, like you're not even here."

"What are you two talking about?" Tully said, not taking her eyes from the display.

"See? You have to command her attention, my friend," Padalmo said.

"His culture's attitude toward interpersonal relations," Moses said in English.

"Mmmhm," Tully said absent-mindedly.

"Why don't you try to woo her, eh?" Padalmo said.

"I don't know what that means," Moses said.

"Convince her to take an interest in you. Invoke infatuation."

Moses shook his head and looked at his feet.

"Come now, even the seeders must have poetry, songs, art. Write her a poem about her beauty. Compare her hair to fire," Padalmo scratched his chin. "Perhaps she wouldn't like that. Or talk about her freckles, or... whatever someone would find attractive in her."

Moses raised his head. "Does this mean you don't think she's attractive?"

"Everyone has different tastes, my friend; don't ever let another man's opinion on a woman change your own. We're not children anymore." Padalmo leaned back in the chair and put his hands behind his head, smiling slightly.

Moses laughed at that. "In many ways, I am still a child. I don't have any idea how to do those things... nor should I try. Not with Tully."

"And why is that?"

"She is the granddaughter of the chieftain," Moses said. He glanced over at Tully at work. "I... don't think... I'm not really part of the clan, or an ally, or useful in any capacity. Macbeth would never allow it."

"Ah, forbidden love," Padalmo said. "I could teach you a thing or two about *that*. Clandestine affairs are my specialty."

"He'd blast me out of the airlock," Moses said.

Padalmo leaned forward and smiled broadly. "Doesn't it just make you want her more?"

Moses stared back at him for a long moment, then answered quietly, "Yes."

Padalmo chuckled. "Of course it does. You can use that, you know. Women are infatuated with forbidden love as much as men."

"You seem much less morally upstanding than I expected a prophet to be."

PROPHET OF THE GODSEED

"Good attempt at changing the subject."

"When you two are done grunting," Tully said, looking at Moses, "I'd like to tap into your implants. I have an idea, but it will probably require your hardware, or a close emulation of it."

"Will you be able to see my data streams?" Moses said in English.

"Of course. That's the point," Tully said.

Moses turned to Padalmo and said in his language, "We must stop this conversation now. We can speak more later, but say nothing of it again until I say."

"Very well, my friend," Padalmo said.

*

Moses waited patiently as Tully connected several multi-pin adapters to the external part of his cerebral implants, and then attached several fiber-optic interface cables to the adapters. She opened up a task window on her display and watched as flurries of code flew by. She moved that over and brought up on the right hand of the screen another task window, displaying images and lines of words among jumbled bits of undecipherable data. Moses watched the words carefully, hoping that he did not unconsciously think of his conversation with Padalmo, and thus make requests of the planet's translation matrix that would expose the things about which he had been talking. Somehow, the thought of Tully knowing what he thought and how he felt seemed a terrifying proposition.

"No need to get so tense," Tully said. She smiled and placed a hand on Moses's forearm. "I'm not concerned with what you're thinking, and I'm not probing your dreams. I'm only trying to evaluate the means by which your implants are interfacing with the network below. The means, not the content."

"I know," Moses said. "It's just... different now, having had privacy. It's something I value now, I suppose."

"It appears you've done something to make her take an interest in you," Padalmo said, smiling.

Moses quickly looked at the screen to see the words sent and returned in translation. He swallowed.

"Interesting," Tully said. "The routing services for the internet are highly localized; there doesn't seem to be a central registry. How did you originally find the address for this translation matrix?"

"I, uh..." Moses stammered as he watched Tully. "I don't really know. It seemed to do it on its own. I didn't even really think about it."

Tully scratched her head and scrolled through the transmission logs that were being recorded from Moses's implants. "Maybe they sort things based on context-relations prior to formalized address requests."

"What?" Moses said. Padalmo raised an eyebrow to him.

"Basically, you aren't asking any server for translations, you are just sending out raw data. Somewhere on their net, that data is assumed to have a particular purpose, and is processed that way. It's actually really interesting, especially since it isn't going through any sort of central server registry. It's spread out across thousands of servers, who exchange information like peers."

"Peers?" Moses said. "I thought peers were people."

"It's just a networking term," Tully said.

"Sorry, I haven't received any training on networking yet."

"You should. You are, in a very literal sense, built for computer networking. Maybe when the ship-fleet is under way again I can find some time to give you the basics, eh?"

"You... want to spend time with me?" Moses said.

"Sure," Tully said with a shrug. "I don't have much experience as a teacher, but-" She cut off and looked intently at the screen.

"But what?" Moses said.

"Peers. Something you said. Can I take control of your implants for a few moments?"

"Um, sure," Moses said.

His mind was flooded with confusing signals and images. Numbers repeated, and noise filled his ears. He flinched and shut his eyes, then put his hands over his ears. The random data flooding his mind became unbearable, and he felt sick.

"Sorry," Tully said. "I'll make it quick."

Moses forced his eyes open and tried to listen to his surroundings, finding that it put the noise of whatever Tully was doing into a sort of background layer. He focused on Tully's face, then her eyes, which darted back and forth as she took in the display. Moses focused on the trembling reflection of the lighted display on her blue irises. The visuals and sounds became like something seen in his periphery. The noise was intense, but it was still somehow buried behind the soft clicking of keys and humming of fans.

The data stopped. Tully cocked her head as she looked at Moses, who remained staring at her eyes, looking almost catatonic.

"Ok?" She said, raising an eyebrow.

"Oh thank God," Moses said. He closed his eyes and shook his head. "That was a rather unpleasant experience."

"Really? I was just pinging some of the addresses that your implants were accessing, sending out packets of random data to see where they went. It shouldn't have done anything."

"Yes, well..." Moses tried to focus on the moment, and the silence. "My implants translate network data into messages my brain can understand. Random data creates noise. Visual, audio, noise. No smells though. Or tastes. Or touches." Moses sighed.

"Sorry Moses," Tully said. "I didn't think it would bother you. I won't do it again."

"You can try again, if it helps you," Moses said. "I can manage."

"It's alright. I found out enough, I think, and I can emulate your networking capabilities if I need to." She leaned back in her chair. "It's like you said. The peers are people."

PROPHET OF THE GODSEED

"I don't understand," Moses said.

"The networking peers, the interconnected servers, are end users. They are people with implants. At least half of them are. Their network, as near as I can tell, in a vast de-centralized peer-focused internet. Requests for information, searches, whatever, appear to occur through a cascade system, where the info is sent from one user to several until relevant bits are retrieved, sent back, then re-assembled. The internet *is* the people."

"Why am I a peer?" Moses said. "I'm from Earth."

"Just coincidence," Tully said. "Your implants operate partially on a compatible wavelength, and you encode linguistic data with the same binary structure, coincidentally again. Everything else you send out dissipates because it makes no sense to anyone on the network. I mean, this is surprisingly rare. It's also very, very interesting, because on Earth, near as we can tell from you, information isn't stored locally; it's stored on separate computers directed by the Omni-core. On this planet, data stays here." She tapped the side of Moses's head.

"So I'm communicating with other people?" Moses said. "Are they aware of my thoughts?"

"Maybe, maybe not," Tully said. "Most of what you send out would be useless noise for them. I imagine that their hardware contains some sort of buffer to filter things before they reach cognitive levels of a peer. Maybe the whole thing happens subconsciously for these people, and they aren't aware of any data requests. That seems the most efficient to me, but who knows?"

Moses thought for a moment, and then said. "How shall we disable their network, as the captain asked?"

"Good question," Tully said.

"Thank you."

"Just an expression, Moses."

Moses cocked his head, confused.

CHAPTER 7
Fire Ark

"The Dark Side faction seems to be overwhelming the military of Padalmo's faction at every point," Anders said. He stood in front of the huge display, showing several live orbital images of the mostly empty agricultural zones outside the planet's major metropolitan areas. The computer colored life signs in vivid red, with active machines a pale blue. The troops from the dark side were colored often in shades of violet, marked by the signals their implants sent out constantly.

"Except here," Claribel said, pointing at a narrow point between two mountainous regions. Red and purple dots piled on top of one another, with sparse reserves behind.

"That is the pass to Pana'Chu, as Padalmo described it. A natural bottleneck. The fighting there will be fierce and probably stalemated."

"Why did they choose to attack there?" Claribel cued through several other images. "All the other battlefields are in open spaces."

"I hypothesize that the Darksiders are attacking the pass for two reasons. First, because it is the shortest route to Pana'Chu, which seems to be the most politically important of the major city-states. Second, because the Faithful have fortified that area and are expecting an attack there. It will keep them occupied and distracted, while the blitzkrieg comes from the sea adjacent to the city."

"That analysis appeals to me," Claribel said. She enlarged the view of the battlefield in the mountain pass. "Occupy their military so the real attack is nearly unopposed. And, if you are successful, you have captured Pana'Chu regardless." She zoomed in, to where she could see a group of soldiers shooting each other, snuffing out red lights and leaving poorly camouflaged bodies on the ground. She zoomed back out and looked at Anders. "The horror of war is a good motivator, but bad for clear thinking."

"The greatest commanders have led from the battleground," Anders said. "Horror and inspiration are the same."

"Hmn," Claribel said. She flipped over to a view of a battle in some orchards and wheat fields, south of another city. She backed up the footage by an hour and watched the troop movements in a sped-up repetition of the ongoing battle. "Notice how coordinated the Darksider attack is." She moved the recording forward and backward. "I assume that Padalmo's faction is using radios to communicate, but their enemies clearly are more efficient. They are always on the offensive, and are moving past and beyond troop lines quickly and without hesitation. Normally, farmland makes for a terrible battlefield. Too open. Too easy to see and attack at distance. Too easy to dig in and too little cover during attack. The Darksiders chose this battlefield, and they are winning."

"It's their implants," Anders said.

"Yes, it is. This is a world-wide coordinated attack. They don't need a general on the battlefield barking orders, or a campaign supreme commander directing armies. Every unit has all the information of all other units available to it instantly. They are collectively thinking their way to victory."

"I see now," Anders said. He brought up a larger view of several battlefields adjacent to one another. The troops appeared as red and purple blurs on the map. He rewound and sped up the footage. "They are using their transports to deliver equipment, men, and artillery exactly where it is needed, and moving them across fields as one battle goes better and another meets resistance. It's incredibly efficient." Blue dots flew between the conflicted areas, and as the footage sped up, they became a blurry line connecting the two.

"Do you think they will be successful in capturing the nuclear arsenal before the Faithful can invoke an apocalypse?" Claribel said.

"We predict victory in about two hours, an incredibly short battle. They are coordinating so all forces arrive in the nuclear military facilities at the same time."

"That may still be too slow. One city could step out from the others and initiate."

"An individual city will not have the payload necessary to cause nuclear winter, according to our evaluations."

"Many millions will still be killed," Claribel said. "I don't want to take that risk. I want to pull the plug on this attack *now*."

"We'll be supporting one faction over the other, directly," Anders said. "We don't usually do that."

"I know, but I feel I must make an exception here," Claribel said. "When one faction has a religious belief in annihilation, you can't assume that peace will be brokered eventually. Let's hope Tully can come up with a means of terminating their cybernetic net."

"I suggest a contingency," Anders said. "We have our fighters prepped in the bays of *Icarus* proper. We also have battle probes. We believe they are using ballistic missiles for payload delivery. If they launch, we can destroy the missiles in flight from orbit."

"And irradiate thousands of square miles of populated land?" Claribel said. "That's if the bombs don't explode and cook everyone below."

"It's a contingency, Claire, not 'plan A.' Irradiated land can be evacuated. People can be treated for radiation sickness. If a missile hits a city, it's a sure thing. All of the cities have millions of people living in them."

"You'll need father's say-so," Claribel said. "I don't have the capacity or the authority to deploy weapon systems. Our time is short. Very short." She opened up a channel with Tully. "Tully, I need you to double-time on your network neutralization measures."

"What?" Tully said. "I didn't hear my com ring."

"You're not the only one around here who knows how to get around com security," Claribel said. "You have..." she looked at Anders who held up nine fingers. "Ninety minutes for your plan to implementation-ready."

"Ninety minutes!" Tully said. "I thought I'd have at least a day. What's the rush?"

"War," Claribel said. "Whatever you've got, we're making an attempt in ninety minutes."

"Do you still have Padalmo with you?" Anders said. Claribel frowned at him.

"Yes, why?" Tully said.

He looked at Claribel. "I just thought of another contingency. A good one. Maybe not 'Plan A,' but definitely 'Plan B.'"

*

Malcolm Macbeth stood at the end of a steel walkway, surveying the planet which loomed before him and the rest of his crew, nearly filling the huge HUD-integrated windows that made up Macbeth's bridge. The desert the planetsider had called Drogathalum stood out in stark detail, a sea of sand next to a boiling sea that covered nearly half of the planet, bathed eternally in the light of the nearby star. Clouds lifted themselves up and raced over to the habitable zone before falling to ice in the darkness beyond.

Terranostra was a chaotic, timeless planet, without semblance of cycle, season, or even day. Weather was intense and constant. Somehow, the people on the planet had managed to do much more than eke out a meager existence. They had thrived, building grand cities, inventing new technology, and forming ordered societies. This feat was even more impressive with the knowledge of the planet's nuclear cataclysm, which had erased all of the technological and social advantages that the clan had left them millennia before.

The survivors had rebuilt, and from nothing they had evolved so far as to be in danger of technological singularity, the ultimate death of humanity that had made the human home world a horrific monument to collective thought and control. That impressed even Macbeth, who had overseen the birth and rebirth of countless seeded civilizations in his lifetime.

He watched now with careful attention to detail as each sector of the ancient map recovered from the quantum gate was overlaid with the live view of the Terranostra's sunward side. He saw ancient structures in a pale green light, places of work and life even in the inhospitable desert that had been utterly erased in the time since the cataclysm, beaten down by the raging weather and swallowed by the shifting sands. It filled him with sadness; he would remember this perspective, and these events, in hope of preventing them in other worlds.

"Timothy. Bring up that last sector on my screen."

"Aye, sir," Timothy said.

A large detail of the desert sector filled Malcolm's large display at the helm. He shifted the image around until he saw something in the ancient map overlay. It

PROPHET OF THE GODSEED

was faint, but clear: A large rounded protrusion in the sand, a short distance away from what was once likely a mining establishment.

"Give me a targeted scan of this point," Macbeth said, pointing to the protrusion.

"Yes sir," Vanessa said.

"Sir, that looks like a rock," Jon said. "When you look at the original image, in color, even more so."

"It likely was – or is – a rock," Macbeth said. "But rocks protruding from these sands have deep roots. It makes a good place to build a bomb shelter."

"Sir?" Jon said. "I'm not sure I understand. Not to question, but aren't we looking for a stockpile?"

"I spent some time talking to the planetsider," Macbeth said. "He talked about a 'Fire Ark.' I believe it was actually a large shelter which allowed its inhabitants to wait out the nuclear inferno. If I were mining heavy elements in the desert, I would probably pick a similar type of structure to a bomb shelter to stockpile the raw materials. A huge slab of granite is ideal for blocking radiation, both radiation going out, and radiation coming in. At the very least, if we can find something other than the gate that remains from the first society, it may contain important information. Was that enough explanation for you?"

"Uh, yes sir," Jon said. "I... did not mean to infer I didn't trust you. It's just..."

"Never pass up an opportunity to question a superior, especially if you don't understand his motives,

Jon," Macbeth said. "Besides, I needed to explain it to myself."

"Trying to work through a hunch, sir?" John said.

"Hunches are hard to justify, but still require it," Macbeth said. "I never act on a whim. Neither should you."

"Sir, I'm assembling some data for you," Vanessa said. Macbeth strode past Jon on his way to Vanessa's station. She brought up a large detail of the area, and then separated the ancient map and the modern orbital view of the planet. "I'm detecting a large amount of ferrous materials here." The display lit up with a purple splotch, though the visual image showed nothing but sand dunes.

"How deep?"

"Looks to be about four meters. Not very deep at all. These dunes could be a rather recent feature, given the weather systems on this planet."

"Gravitational analysis?"

"Still processing," Vanessa said. "But the iron alone should hint at something man-made. There's solid iron down there. Wait-" She brought up another color on the screen. "There's a lot of lead in there, it looks like. Gravitational analytics can't seem to pierce that layer of heavy metal without some more time."

"Keep on it," Macbeth said. "For my money, that's a radiation shelter. The lead could be added protection, or it could be the remnants of decayed fissile material. We'll have to go take a closer look."

"A closer look?" Vanessa said.

PROPHET OF THE GODSEED

Macbeth opened a com channel. On a nearby terminal "Bertrand, are you standing about idle?"

"Beats pretending to look busy, Mac," a voice sounded back. An old face framed with a grey beard stepped into view. "Sir."

"Good. Prep a transport, and put a digger on it, ASAP."

"They're all already prepped, hence why I'm standing about idle," Bertrand said. "I'll be in the launch bay, at your leisure."

"Thanks, Bert. Jon, you have the helm, and command," Macbeth said, looking to the young helmsman. "Timothy, draft whoever you need to continue your work. Vanessa, you're with me."

"Excellent," Vanessa said, smiling. She went slack-faced as Macbeth leered at her.

"It's okay to be excited about opportunity," he said, smirking. Vanessa nodded and began collecting her things from the surface of the workstation.

Macbeth's personal com rang.

"What is it, Anders?"

"Our department needs say-so on a few things," he said. "But mostly, I wanted to discuss a plan I had in mind, as a contingency, that utilizes Padalmo."

*

The multipurpose digger, for its rather modest size, was a mammoth when fulfilling its purpose. Slowly it ground its way through layers of sand, hardened nearly to stone, using an array of diamond grinding tools that pulverized stone superheated by the digger's multiphasic lasers. What erupted from the long carbonized chute at the rear of the digger was a mixture of dust and debris that was nearly on fire, like volcanic ash.

Malcom Macbeth stood back from the digger, watching carefully the operation behind dark tinted goggles and a thin heat-shielded hat. He made notes on his tablet, looking around occasionally to check the status of the armed security specialists that lined the nearby dunes. He looked up again as Vanessa approached, heading away from the multipurpose digger.

"We've hit more solid rock," she said, handing over her own tablet, with read-outs of the digger's progress and the on-board analysis tools. "It's heavy-laden with metallic elements, especially iron. It's denser than granite, but softer because of its iron-oxide content, but it is less dense than basalt should be."

"No conclusiveness as to whether this was once an ocean, then," Malcolm said.

"No, sir," she said. "Pardon me, sir, but does that matter?"

"Not really," Malcolm said. "It's puts things in perspective though. Geologic time – *real deep time* – exists on a scale even beyond us. It's good to be reminded of how young humanity is sometimes."

They both turned as the steady whine of an approaching transport began to penetrate the deep, low rumbling of the digger. It was one of the transports held on Grey Wing, smaller, more nimble, and less adaptable than the main shuttles on *Icarus's* main section. The blue glow of the engine exhaust was drowned in the ever-white of the desert, making the transport look like a moving dead husk. A reflection off the cockpit's corundum glass temporarily blinded Malcolm and Vanessa as the ship turned and presented a side. It hovered in mid-air and slowly lowered itself to the uneven sand, sliding downhill slightly before resting.

The door in the center of the transport slid open. Anders and Moses appeared, donning long coats and wide-brimmed hats, similar to what the planetsider had worn when he was rescued. They turned back to the open door and looked at a pensive Padalmo, his hat held in his hands, hesitating as if he were about to jump off a cliff. Moses gestured him over. Finally, he took a step out of the vehicle and followed Anders and Moses to the chieftain.

"Took you long enough," Malcolm said, smirking.

"I thought it would be prudent to stay above the detection range of the natives," Anders said.

Malcolm gave an approving grunt and nod.

"I thought you were calling me down to implement my plan," Anders said, looking around at the empty desert.

"For now, that remains a contingency, and one I still do not wish to pursue. Interacting with planetary politics is dangerous business, even more so when you mix in religion." Malcolm looked to Padalmo.

"He *is* the prophet."

"He'll only be such if he must be," Malcolm said. "For now, I need his perspective on this. It is, I believe, his Fire Ark."

"We're almost to a safe probing distance," Vanessa said. She pointed to the digger, which continued its downward descent.

Padalmo said something and then wrapped his face with a cloth, then covering his eyes with his goggles.

Malcolm looked to Moses. "Well?"

"Sorry sir, I'm getting a lot of lag out here. He says that you should all cover your faces. The sand will kill you to breathe it over-long."

"Better take his advice," Malcolm said. After wrapping his own face, Anders handed the chieftain and Vanessa each a long piece of cloth that was like light linen. Malcolm quickly wrapped his mouth and nose. "I suppose I over-estimated Moses's usefulness, this time."

"Tully won't be happy to hear that," Anders said. "I practically had to pry him away from her."

"She'll manage without. She always does," Malcolm said.

"Let's step back for a few minutes, shall we?" Vanessa said, staring at her tablet. "I think I'm punching through something. Old steel, maybe. It could be dangerous."

***

Bright lights turned on, shining down onto iron platforms that had not been set upon since the antiquity of Terranostra. Motes of silica dust fell from the opening, illuminated by crisscrossing beams, searching for purchase in the vast cavern.

"Do we have a ladder?" Anders said. He pulled away the cloth that made up his dust mask and smelled the air. It was stale, but felt fresh enough to breathe.

"Here," Moses said.

Anders took the bundled up cylinder from Moses and placed it where the rock suddenly ended and became a thick wall of iron. The device whirred to life, drilling holes in the iron and thrusting bolt holds·deep into the wall. Anders pressed a button and a long chain of rungs, made of a light titanium alloy, pushed themselves into the depths. After a few seconds, the bottom of the ladder struck steel, creating a booming sound that resonated in the abyss. Anders pushed another button and the ladder began to push away from the wall, becoming a long row of narrow-stepped stairs. The cylinder that had formerly held the portable stairs split apart, allowing them to descend.

"Padalmo," Malcom said from behind. "It is your holy place. You should step first."

Moses translated after a delay of a few seconds and the youth stepped forward. He took off his hat and kneeled down, praying silently. He stood up and spoke softly.

Moses translated his quiet words, "Long have we sought the fire ark. Long have we sought to make the holy into the real and touchable. Here it is, at last: the truth of our faith, though I think it shall be a truth other than what we expected."

They shuffled down the narrow stairs, one by one, following Padalmo. The beams of flashlights wagged, showing walls of dark steel that were mostly unmarked. In some places, corrosion had gained a foothold over the ancient seal of the metal, and rust had worked deep pits into the carbon-iron alloy. Piles of red dust sat upon the floor, undisturbed for an age. Their steps echoed back through an endless vertical space as they stepped out onto the platform, groaning slightly under the weight of the crew as much as under the weight of years.

Padalmo sighed. He spoke slowly and quietly.

"What's he saying?" Malcolm said, looking to Moses, who was looking over a rail into the dark, which swallowed the beam of his flashlight.

"I seem to have lost my network connection," Moses said. "Perhaps we could assemble a transponder up above, to relay my signal."

"Vanessa, is that doable?" Malcolm said.

"I have a network bridge in the transport. I should be able to assign it to Moses's implant frequencies," Vanessa said.

"Good," Malcolm said. "Bring some floodlights down while you're at it."

Vanessa hurried back up the portable stair, her steps changing from a cacophonous rattle to a gentle thud as she reached the rock above.

"I wonder if the lights still work," Anders said, working his way along the wall and away from the entrance.

"Judging by the corrosion, I wouldn't put a stake on it," Malcolm said, following Anders.

"The gate was still functional," Anders said.

"That's because I made it to endure. I don't know who made this place. We are also not in the vacuum of space. There are always forces at work on a planet, grinding everything a man makes back into dust."

"I find it remarkable how intact it is," Moses said, flashing his light along the solid, still grey rails of the platform. "The steel supports our weight. After two thousand years, that has to count for something."

"Here," Anders said. He shined his light on a switch box. He opened it up and toggled a few switches. Nothing happened. "No power reserves left, of course. I'm too used to our own technology."

"There's a little," Moses said. "I can hear when you flip the switch, a small amount of current."

"You can hear that?" Anders said, flipping a switch.

"Um... yes," Moses said. "I hear white noise."

"He's picking up interference on his implants," Malcolm said. "These lights are powered by a simple circuit and some fluorescent ballasts, putting out some EM interference Moses can pick up. Knowing that, the preservation here is indeed quite remarkable."

Footsteps heralded Vanessa's return, carrying a wheeled cart full of equipment.

"I activated the network bridge," she said.

"Yes, I can hear it now," Moses said.

"I also brought some compact power cells, in case any electronics might still be functional below."

"I was about to send you back up to get some," Malcolm said.

"I prefer to be ahead of a superior's demands," Vanessa said.

"I see that," Malcolm said. "Let's get a few lights up here, then we'll head down. Anyone scared of ancient crypts?" Silence answered him, and he clapped his hands.

Vanessa and Anders worked at putting up the massive floodlights along the platform, which proved to be but the top of many steel platforms connected by stairs and ladders, descending into an abyss below them. Once the floodlights were up and pointed down, Malcolm Macbeth and his company were able to see that the walls were entirely black, which had given them a false sense of space. The platforms stood at one end of what was a vertical shaft some ten meters square, with the other side containing an elevator assembly and sealed doors. The elevator reached its top floor several meters below them, with the gear assembly occupying the same horizontal space as the party's entry point.

"Is it all you expected, Padalmo?" Macbeth said, nodding to Moses to translate.

"Artists over the years have painted many renditions of the Fire Ark," Padalmo said through Moses. "All of them seemed to imagine a ship, like a boat, impervious to fire, riding the storms of God himself."

Malcolm nodded. "In a way, it is a boat, sailing the sea of sand, as you called it, which in its burning was safest from the nuclear inferno that destroyed the men of old."

"Drogathalum," Padalmo said. "It's meaning is enhanced, lord."

"Let us see what we can see," Malcolm said, and gestured for Padalmo to descend the next set of stairs. "Below are memories that even I cannot fathom. You must be my guide."

Padalmo nodded and began the descent, steps echoing on the ancient metal steps of a long staircase. He passed through several levels, ignoring the sealed doors and the archeological secrets they undoubtedly held. They reached the bottom of the shaft, which seemed about forty meters deep. Padalmo paused and looked about in the dim gloom. The air felt dry and stagnant, yet thick with the weight of years. When they moved, they kicked up piles of dust that colored the light beams like fog.

"Here," Vanessa said, and handed Padalmo a flashlight. The youth used it to look around, and seeing a large, high-ceilinged round corridor, led the group through it.

They entered an open hall, the flashlight beams finding countless pieces of electronics and chairs. Vanessa removed another battery-operated floodlight from the cart and lit it up, illuminating the vast space. It was a packed room, lined with what looked like computer stations and displays. A few still clung to the walls where they were mounted, once, but many more had fallen or sat askew. Chairs, their coverings rotted away in places, sat jumbled in different areas.

"So strange," Padalmo said, absent-mindedly.

*

Dimlo grimaced as he paused the stream of incoming reports. He read the line twice, and then dialed in the radio. There was silence.

He stood up and shouted "Father!" in a voice loud enough and clear enough to turn almost all the heads in the war room, a place both busy and eerily quiet. Imalmo took a last glance at a display and strode over to his son. He wore now all his medals in his dress uniform, and looked the part of Highlord more than he ever had before.

"What is it?"

Dimlo pointed to one of the reports on screen. "There's been an attack at the estate. The radio is dead out there."

Imalmo's brow creased ever so slightly. "Are you sure?"

"Yes, but how? All the forces of the enemy are entrenched in the pass. There's nobody in the open plains."

"Nobody but our allies," Imalmo said. His face looked grave.

While Dimlo pondered these words, the radio leapt to life.

"Hello! Hello! Is there anybody out there?" Dimlo immediately recognized the voice of Fala, Padalmo's mother.

PROPHET OF THE GODSEED

"Yes! Yes!" Dimlo said. "This is Dimlo!"

"Thank the Seeders," Fala said.

"Is Imad there?" Dimlo asked.

"No, he went out to fight. They are attacking us. They... aren't the enemy," Fala said. Static filled the channel for a few seconds before clearing.

"Hold tight," Dimlo said. "I'll pull you out of there as soon as I can."

"Please..." Fala's voice faded to static, and the channel died totally.

"Jafta has moved in our empty pocket," Imalmo said.

"Just as we always thought they would," Dimlo said. "Bastards!"

"Malalko has revealed himself to be a traitor to the prophet," Imalmo said.

"We must send a detachment there," Dimlo said. "I'll pull out the 5th and have them hit it."

"No," Imalmo said. "It is already lost. And we cannot spare any men from the front. This was always the gambit."

Dimlo slammed his hand on the console, and the metal rang loudly in the chamber. He thought of his brothers and sisters, dying to Jaftan bullets, and almost wanted to cry. He felt his father's hand rest lightly on his shoulder.

"His reward will be justly earned," Imalmo said. The Highlord turned and addressed a nearby man. "Is the brilliance prepared, commander Forlano?"

"Yes sir," the man said, turning to his station. "I have full control. The others have not betrayed us."

Imalmo caught the eye of his son. "Malalko was right to be wary of spies, but he was not wary enough." He turned back to the commander. "So let it be done, Forlano. Let the memory of Malalko's name be swept away like ashes outside of the ark."

Drawn from the Water

16 months earlier, ship time

THE DOOR FELL inward, floating and tumbling for a few seconds before crashing into a corroded beam of steel, pitted and rusted, then ricocheting off of a dead terminal. The darkness was total inside the derelict craft, and only the light streaming in from the transport provided any illumination. Anders, Tully, and Randall turned on the lights attached to the top of their environmental suits. Dust filled the beams in strange patterns amid the zero-g environment. Tully cautiously pushed her head past the airlock and looked down one direction, then the other of the interior, which took the shape of an immense empty hallway that extended to what looked like infinity.

"Spooky," she said. The tremble in her voice was amplified by the com.

Anders pulled himself in and floated toward the panel across from the airlock. He shined his headlamp on it. A layer of ice was busy forming on the ancient screen. He pushed his gloved hand over it, revealing nothing but darkness. He punched a few nameless keys, but nothing happened. His breath seemed oppressively loud, and he could almost hear his blood rushing in his ears, along with his own pulse. The craft was totally silent, and any ambient noise was further muffled by his environmental suit.

"It's dead," he said into his radio.

Tully, behind him, said, "Looks like it's in bad shape. It's holding pressure, but not much else." She had a datapad open and was using it to scan her surroundings. Multihued light colored the interior of the semicircular hallway. Anders could see no doors or offshoots from the hallway in either direction. Ice from latent moisture clung to steel supports and clean white plastic that lined the floor and walls. Liquid water clouded the chamber, slowly gathering into larger spheres before beginning to freeze again.

"Wet in here," Randall said.

"Not that surprising," Anders said. "We keep a relative humidity in our cabins for comfort. It just doesn't precipitate out like this because we keep it warm." Anders floated down the long deck, shining his lamp here and there. More terminals stood blank and empty around him. He paused for a moment to look at one, which had black marks around a large central vent.

"Must have been one of the power centers," Tully said, pulling forward along the beams of one of the walls. "If you want the data center, it's probably not on this deck. I would guess these are system terminals."

PROPHET OF THE GODSEED

"Still worth a look if we can power them up." Anders pried off the vent and peered inside. White plastic was blackened where a small fire had lit itself before quickly dying in the cold and low-oxygen atmosphere. "I'll come back."

He pushed off and followed Tully down the dark corridor. Randall floated along beside him, taking it in.

"How old do you think it is? It looks like a miracle it's holding together at all. This corrosion..." He drew his finger over a steel support and brought back a streak of red rust. "Maybe the metal has been sinking the oxy?"

"Could be, if they don't have a fusion plant online to make more, or are using tanks. It's funny – the plastic parts are incredibly well preserved."

"No UV light in this windowless tomb," Randall said. "There's some hatches." He pointed toward an intersection a few dozen yard ahead. There were three hatches: One going forward, one in what looked like the floor, and one in what should have been the ceiling. Tully was already working on the lower one, turning a large wheel.

"Hold on," Anders said. He pulled a flashlight from his belt and banged against the steel hatch. It echoed beyond, though the sound was muffled by his sealed helmet. "Sounds pressurized, go ahead."

Tully continued turning the wheel, her legs wrapped around a rail for stability, until it wouldn't budge. Randall moved up beside her and added his own leverage, and with a loud grinding, the hatch released and moved inward. Anders shined his light into the darkness beyond. Mist filled the chamber. His mask fogged slightly.

"Whoa," Randall said.

"It's warmer in there," Tully said. "Maybe there's a power plant nearby."

"Where were those lingering heat areas?" Anders asked.

Tully pulled up her datapad again and flipped through a screen. "This corridor, I think. About forty meters away."

"Then let's have a look," Anders said. He pushed himself into the new corridor, which was wider than the last. It too was lined in white paneled plastic. Terminals stood in odd positions on every wall and surface.

"They must not have equipped this ship with artificial gravity after all," Randall said.

"Maybe they did, but used it like the Hosokawa, gravitizing the ceiling and using all three dimensions for work space," Anders said.

"I heard we're meeting up with them again, yeah?" Tully said.

"Keep your head in the game, Tull," Anders said.

"Right," Tully said. "This panel here is a bit warm." She nodded to a multi-screen terminal with a fixed seat, mounted to a surface opposite an identical station, like two objects mirrored above and below. Anders pulled himself into the seat and tried a few buttons.

"It's an English keyboard," he said. "Very interesting. Still warm like you said. Dead now, though. Maybe I can run some energy through it locally. Randall, give me some more light."

Randall pulled around and turned on his handheld lamp, filling the small section of the empty craft with white light. Anders felt around the edge of the top panel and began prying off the top. The plastic cracked and came away in pieces, revealing a silicon logic board filled with daughter cards of unknown purpose.

"That's one way to do it," Tully said. She pulled herself around the back and pulled off another plastic panel, sending it floating off into the darkness.

"Let me know if you see something that looks like a power supply or a transformer."

"Here," Tully said. "There's a power conduit running into some transformers back here."

Anders pulled a universal battery from his belt and floated it toward Tully.

"See if you can run that into the transformers. It should automatically match the current. If we can find a junction we may be able to get the whole system back online."

"Nifty," Tully said. She squeaked as a clang sounded in the darkness reverberating through the environmental suits. Randall flinched and found himself tumbling backward, searching his belt for his gamma burner. He found it and caught himself with a rail, then held his weapon forward. The light beams from his helmet seemed swallowed up in the misty, foggy cabin. He could only see a few yards ahead through the moisture.

"Relax," Anders said. "It was just that panel bouncing off of something."

"I'm going to go check it out," Randall said.

"Negative," Anders shot back. "No separation. We all go or we all stay. That's an order."

"Let's go," Tully said. "Let's get out of here."

"Not yet," Anders said. "Let's see if we can get this panel online"

Tully stared out into the dark fog for a long moment, and then nodded. "Right."

The terminal sprang to life, and white letters flitted over black screens.

"Looks like it's going to boot awhile, LT," Randall said. "Let's see what that damn noise is so I can sleep before I die."

"Alright," Anders said. "I have other power supplies. Let's keep moving. Tully, keep your scanner running."

"Range is a bit limited with this moisture."

"Understood."

They pushed themselves forward as the computer terminal behind them clicked and hummed, projecting ghosts of characters on the white walls. A few meters away the darkness crept in again, oppressive and omnipresent. Anders had to repeatedly wipe moisture from his glass face mask, and his breath began to feel hot and loud again.

"There it is," Randall said. He pushed off a wall and grabbed the panel Tully had spent flying. He looked around and said, "I wonder what it bounced off of."

"You all there?" Willem's voice said through the com.

"Yes," Anders said. "What's the problem?"

"Nothing, I just lost your signals for a minute there. That hull has some insulating properties, I think."

"We'll switch to multiband," Anders said. "But if you lose us again, we're probably fine. This ship has held together this long. I think it can handle a few hours more. Don't, under any circumstances, switch to unsecured transmission types. I'd like to keep at least the spirit of the old man's orders intact. This ship might not be broadcasting, but that doesn't mean it can't attack our networks."

"Copy."

Anders pushed forward past Anders into the foggy dark, pulling himself along an insulated conduit. The casing cracked under his hands as he went, sending shivers to his spine. Tully and Randall followed close behind. A cracking and hissing sound erupted from the conduit. Anders looked back to see sparks flying from a few places. A nearby terminal, hidden in the dark, leapt to life and cast ghostly beams of light through the mist.

"Looks like your power source is working," Tully said.

"Not well enough," Randall said. "These light fixtures are still dead." He tapped a clear plastic panel above them.

"Their bulbs and diodes probably burned out hundreds of years ago," Tully said.

"Good point," Randall said. They continued following Anders down the hall, this time pushing in between terminals and other hardware fixtures, steering clear of the conduit. After a minute or so, Anders came upon something that scattered the light from his flashlight back to him. He flinched and adjusted his light as he approached.

"It's glass of some sort," he said.

"Look at them all," Randall said. He pulled his extra light from his belt and sent a bright white beam through the mist. Rows of round glass tubes lined the walls of the corridors, leaning towards one another. A few colored lights blinked in control consoles, but they all stood dark and frosted over with moisture and ice.

"Stasis pods," Anders said. "Necessary from a ship this slow. Are any of them still hot?"

"I think so," Tully said. "The mist is scattering things."

Anders pulled up to the closest pod and ran his hands over the glass. His headlamp cut through and revealed the remains of a person, once desiccated into a mummy, but now suffering new rot in the wet cabin. The lifeless lips were drawn tight over teeth that protruded from withered gums and bone. Bony fingers rested on clothing that shone white in a few places where the wet corpse dust had not muted it to a grey. The hair still clung to the scalp in many places, and the lids of the eyes were open, revealing a chasm of where eyes might once have been, now sunken and wet.

Tully wretched and coughed.

"Hold it together," Anders said. He reached up and snapped a picture with the camera on his helmet. "We're likely to see more." He pushed away from the corpse and began floating down the line of pods. "Let's see if we can find a few that are still sealed up and powered on."

"I'm willing to bet that these had their own redundant auxiliary power," Tully said, trying to hold her words together without another cough. "We could probably use another power supply to get these back online."

"To what end?" Randall said. "Anyone in here that doesn't have power is likely long dead."

"Hold up," Anders said. He paused and shined his light forward. A few meters ahead was a long round piece of glass from a pod, floating peacefully. Anders maneuvered around it. A pod stood just past it, empty and open.

"Shit," Tully said. "Shit! One of them is out and loose in here."

Randall pulled his gamma burner out and crossed it under his light, pointing it out into the misty darkness.

"Calm your nerves," Anders said. "Oxy is low in here. Too low to maintain consciousness. This pod could have already been empty anyway."

"I don't like it," Tully said. "I'm going back."

"No!" Anders said. "No separation. That's an order. Now Tully, check your readings again."

"What?"

"Give me an IR reading, damn it!"

Tully tore her eyes from the darkness and pulled her datapad up again. "There's definitely some residual heat, maybe body head. Um... That area on the right." She pointed and Anders pushed off the empty pod toward a few red lights, shining out like stars in the darkness of the cabin. He pulled up beside it and rubbed the moisture off. A pair of folded dark-skinned hands was underneath. Anders continued working upward. When he got to the face, he found he could not wipe off the fog.

"He's breathing," Anders said. "Quick, Tully, give me an O_2 read."

Tully pointed her datapad at the pod. "Eighteen percent, but dropping rapidly."

"Are we doing this?" Randall removed from his side pouch a portable life support system with an oxygen tank and mask.

"He's alive, so yes," Anders said. He shined his light on the control panel, brushed his gloves over some ancient buttons, and found a long rotary handle. He pulled it out and began turning it. Gas escaped from the seal of the stasis pod, rushing out in a hiss that

PROPHET OF THE GODSEED

sounded loud even in the EV suits. Anders put his fingers under the edge of the glass and tried to lift it up, but it wouldn't fully disengage.

Tully grabbed his arm as he tried to operate the console, still drawing a miniscule amount of power. "Anders, look!"

Anders paused to see the man's face through the partially lifted glass. It was a placid, serene face, but there were long strips of metal emerging from his head in several places where his neural and auditory implants entered his cranium. His eyes fluttered open, and he shook his head in confusion. His hands moved up to the implants, probing and re-probing.

"He's confused," Randall said. "I bet he's trying to connect to his network and failing."

"I might need to power this panel up to get the lid all the way off," Anders said. He pulled in closer and pried open a panel of the pod. He removed another universal power supply and connected it to a transformer. Dim LEDs were replaced with brilliant fluorescent lights as the pod lit up. The man inside howled and covered his eyes. The lid released and flew up, held onto the pod by an ancient rusty hinge. The man inside tumbled forward, his arms flailing. His hoarse voice carried in the dark.

"Quick, grab him!" Randall said, reaching forward and seizing one of the stranger's sleeves. The man recoiled and, without gravity or hold to restrict movement, both of them began to tumble. Randall's helmet hit another pod with a dull thud. He grabbed a nearby rail and recovered.

"Randall! Do you have a sedative?" Tully said, pushing away from the drifting, flailing, screaming man.

"Yes! Let me find it," Randall said as he opened one of his belt pouches. He drew out a stout syringe and pushed toward the man, holding the needle like a dagger.

"No!" Anders said, pulling himself beside Tully. "The oxygen level in here is low, he'll lose consciousness shortly. Don't risk injuring yourselves or tearing your suit."

Randall nodded and waited for the man to stop, but as the moments ticked by, he seemed to continue his raving. As they watched, the lights on either side of them began to flicker back to life. First one pod, then another, lit up with fluorescence, revealing here and there beyond drops of water parts of corpses and ruined clothing.

Tully screamed. Anders turned his head to see yet another person floating toward them, long hair flying about in a yellow storm. Randall let the hypodermic needle go and drew his weapon again. Before he could draw, sparks flew from bursting bulbs, and then the lights around them flickered a few times before dying again.

"Damn it!" Randall yelled, reaching again for his flashlight. "Damn it!"

PROPHET OF THE GODSEED

Anders reached for his own flashlight and shot it out into the mist, searching for the extra person. Tully continued screaming. The flashlight beams crossed and flashed, confusing Anders's sense of space. Tully thrashed and her headlamp swung wildly. Anders turned to see her kicking at a person just outside her reach. The person floated limply. Randall did not fire, but Anders could hear him breathing loudly through the radio.

"She's dead," Randall said. "It's – it was – a woman."

Anders pushed over and shined his light directly on the facedown body. The pale face of a woman, blue eyes half-open in an abyssal stare, greeted him. Tully stopped screaming and started to sob.

"She can't have been dead long," Anders said.

"Probably the low oxy. Where's the other one? The man," Randall said.

Anders swung his light around the outside of the corridor and settled it on the man they had pulled from the stasis pod. His eyes were half shut and he was breathing heavily, still trying to move his arms and legs. Anders pushed off of a console and floated toward the man.

"He's losing consciousness. Get that oxy mask on him, and give him the sedative anyway."

"Aye," Randall said. The two of them worked on the still defiant man, greatly weakened by the atmosphere. Anders held the man's arms as Randall hastily administered a sedative. As he withdrew the hypodermic needle, small drops of blood flew off in tiny spheres of black-red. Randall released the needle, sending it floating, and pushed the oxygen mask onto the man's face. He affixed with an elastic band. The man's brown eyes wandered for a moment, then closed.

"Christ almighty," Anders said. "Let's get this sod off. Tully." He turned to look at his niece, who still stared at the floating body, her mouth agape. "Tully!"

Tully shook her head and helmet as if to snap out of sleep. "Sure thing."

"I didn't give you any orders."

Tully ignored him and scanned the area again with her datapad. "I think he's the only one."

Anders nodded. "Let's get out of here then."

"Thank god," Randall said.

CHAPTER 8
The Citadel

"Captain!"

Claribel tore her eyes away from the display. Usually, she was unwilling to respond to crew demands immediately or with priority, believing that it made her appear weak and went counter to the autonomous paradigm she wished to instill in her inferiors. Something about the tone in the young man's voice told her she should ignore that impulse.

"What is it, Charles?" She said, striding away from the command console and toward the terminal at the end of the row where, Charles, a survey specialist in training, sat staring agape at his display.

"It's gone," he said.

"What's gone?" Claribel said, leaning over to look at his display.

"The Eastern capital, Jafta. All signals are lost. Electronics, life signs, EM from the power grid. It's gone!"

"Let's get a satellite visual on the main," Claribel said. An image filled the central display of the command console, of a spreading, rolling cloud of grey.

"It's spreading rapidly," Charles said. "It looks like a storm cloud."

"It's a firestorm," Claribel said, wide-eyed. "The nuclear war has begun."

"I don't understand," Charles said. "We haven't detected any launches, any power ups... there's no missiles in the sky down there. And why would the Darksiders nuke a city they are trying to invade?"

"We've completely misunderstood the nature of the nuclear threat facing this planet," Claribel said. "It was never about two empires with their missiles pointed at one another. It was one empire, with the nukes pointed at itself. Planted on itself. Mutually assured destruction at the discretion of the destroyed."

"What do we do?" Charles said.

Claribel stood silent for a long moment, watching the destruction of the city below. Millions of lives, lost because they had mis-assessed the reality of the people in this society. Millions of people who could not protest their destruction at the hand of their rulers. Religion, twisted to bring destruction instead of understanding. She felt a terrible weight dragging her shoulders, threatening to pull her down.

"Captain?" her com rang out. It was Jon, Malcolm's favorite helmsman.

"I'm here."

"Did you see what just happened?"

"Yes. We're monitoring the situation."

"The chieftain is out of contact. That means you're in charge of the fleet. Any orders?"

Claribel took a deep breath. There were still lives to be lost, or won. Her mind began racing.

PROPHET OF THE GODSEED

"Keep your fighters in place to take out any nukes that go flying. Just because this city committed suicide doesn't mean ICBMs or other large-scale weapons won't be launched."

"Understood."

"We need to implement Anders's contingency," Claribel said, half to herself.

"Sir, I'm not aware of that contingency," Jon said.

"Do you have Macbeth's last known location?"

"Yes, I'll transmit."

"Thank you." Claribel punched her com. "Tully."

"I saw," Tully said back. "I'm working on a countermeasure as fast as I can, but I can't guarantee anything."

"Do you have a working emulation for Moses's implant frequencies?"

"Yes, that was the first thing I did."

"Good I need you to contact him, now. I'm sending coordinates in case you want to use our high-gain directional com array. Macbeth's com isn't working wherever he is, but Moses's still might."

"Understood," Tully said.

"After that, I need you to implement your countermeasure, as soon as you feel it might work. Time has run out." Claribel looked around her command console. "Somebody get me some damn coffee."

***

A hum filled the air. Lights above blinked, then flickered, then came to unsteady life, putting the room into shades of pale green. Displays and computer terminals sprang to life. On the central, large display, a blinking cursor appeared on a field of black. Padalmo walked forward and stared at it, a look of disbelief on his face. He started at a loud clacking from the wall.

"The air circulators are starting back up," Anders said. Moses, standing nearby, translated for Padalmo.

Macbeth, wiping his hands with a cloth and with Vanessa trailing him, returned to the central room. "Ah, good," he said, seeing the terminal. "Padalmo, what else do your holy texts say about the fire ark?"

Moses began translating, but stopped mid-sentence.

"What is it?" Malcolm said, pulling a ragged chair away from one of the terminals.

"I'm getting a transmission. From Tully."

Macbeth frowned. "What does she want?"

"The war has begun. One of the cities has destroyed itself. Captain Claribel wants Anders's contingency to be implemented immediately."

Malcom chewed his cheek for a moment. "Go. Vanessa and I will try to ply what we can from these computers. Let's hope the ancients didn't make too many revisions to the programing infrastructure we left them with."

Moses nodded and looked to Padalmo. "Prophet, you are needed," he said in Padalmo's language.

"Very well," Padalmo said. "There is little here but ashes. Tell the lord that I do not think he will find what he seeks here."

PROPHET OF THE GODSEED

Moses nodded and told Macbeth. He and Padalmo joined Anders at the entryway to the wide room. They all took a last look around.

"Anders," Macbeth said, gazing hard into his eyes. "Keep yourself safe, son. You're worth more to me than this bloody planet."

Anders nodded, then turned away, Moses and Padalmo following close behind. They began the long ascent up the steel stairs, their echoing footsteps joining the hum of fans and the clicking of keys in the deep.

*

The transport flew low over the countryside, which blurred by in sheets of tan and green. Anders sat at the helm, his jaw clenched. Moses looked out nervously in front of an equally tense Padalmo. The treetops below, each leaning toward the sun hanging eternally above the horizon, rippled with the mass movement of air created by the ship. They looked like waves upon a yellow-green ocean, rolling under an unnatural wind during a sunset that would never end.

The transport rocked slightly as another ground to air missile hit it and exploded in red fire. The ship remained unscathed. Its exterior was protected by a pulsing gravitational barrier a meter or more around the hull that, though without standard mass, acted to external forces like a sheet of thick tungsten. They passed over other missile stations, most unable to fire upon the low-flying and speedy craft.

"The defenses are becoming heavier," Padalmo said. "We are nearing Pana'Chu." Moses translated for Anders.

"Let's hope we are in time," Anders said. "I've never tested our barrier against serious fissile explosions." He pulled up and the transport raced over a series of foothills, dry and free of vegetation in the areas shaded from the eternal sun. A city appeared beside a wide bay, crowded buildings sprawling for miles around looming skyscrapers. The tall buildings all shared a similar design, leaning away from the sun and the origin of storms, and each having a curved surface pointing sunward, like an airfoil. Evidence of fighting showed itself in the sprawling metropolis. Equipment, tanks, and troops could be seen on streets. Smoke curled skyward from suburbs in the surrounding hills, but the city itself remained untouched.

"The enemies are at the gates," Padalmo said. His eyes seemed to be glassed over, almost unseeing, as if his time on *Icarus* had cured him of amazement. "It is as we have feared for so long." He sighed, and then leaned forward in his seat. "The political leaders of the city will now be at the temple citadel." He pointed away from the skyscrapers, to a mass of low buildings near the shoreline of the large bay.

Anders banked the transport to the right as a flurry of ground to air missiles impacted the ship's shield. The flight leveled out, missiles exploding in front of the cockpit and filling their vision with bright, blinding fire whose crackling sound was dissonantly muted.

PROPHET OF THE GODSEED

"Getting some encrypted long-distance com traffic," Moses said, pulling up a read-out from a screen near his seat.

Anders flipped up his own screen and turned loose of the ship controls; the transport continued on its course uninterrupted. "I see," he said. "I'm suddenly glad I did some software updates last week. I'm going to run a decryption package using the stellar nav cores. We won't need them down here anyway. Can you let me know when the computer trips over something coherent?"

"Aye-Aye," Moses said, bringing up the automated hacking program on his own display. "By the way, Tully's countermeasures haven't gone through yet. I can hear the enemy troops' thoughts – their collective thoughts, if I choose."

"Try to keep yourself on silent, or only listen in short bursts," Anders said. "We don't know whether their collective could issue you commands or not."

"I can always choose to disobey, commander," Moses said.

"You sure?"

"It's not like Earth. There, you obey because you don't know any different. Here, these people act with some amount of free will. I can tell they aren't compelling each other, at least, not in the way that you should be worried about. It's more like command on *Icarus,* only, instead of a chieftain, they have the collective will."

"You'll have to tell me more some other time," Anders said, putting his hands back on the transport's controls. "For now, just monitor that decryption."

"Sir, it's already done," Moses said.

Anders shook his head. "That was fast."

Moses looked at his display. "The program says it was a 32 bit dual-key encryption."

"Damn pitiful," Anders said. "Let's hear it."

Moses brought in a live feed of the audio. A cacophony of arguing voices, speaking a language that was unintelligible to Anders, filled the cabin. Padalmo nearly leapt out of his seat, and began talking frantically.

"What the hell are they saying?" Anders said.

"There's too much going on," Moses said. "I can't pick out what any individual is saying."

"What about him?" Anders said, pointing his thumb back to Padalmo, strapped into one of the seats behind the control console.

"He says that it's his father," Moses said. "His father is speaking, I mean."

"Can we broadcast?" Anders said.

Moses nodded. "I can spoof one of the keys and the address, I think. I don't do much of this in the infirmary."

"Let me do it. You can take control of the ship. Keep us low, try not to make our approach too obvious." Anders let go of the controls again and brought his personal display back up. Moses grabbed onto the two-stick controls in front of his own console, and pushed the ship lower, so it was zooming over strange houses and gardens, which flew under them in a blur.

"We should arrive in about 90 seconds," Moses said.

Anders turned and looked back at Padalmo. "You're on." He pointed at his mouth.

"You can speak to your father," Moses said in Padalmo's language.

Padalmo looked stunned for a second. "Father?"

The shouting voices continued.

"Father! It's me, Padalmo! Listen!"

The voices died down to a murmur, and then were silent.

"It's coming from your address," one voice said.

"It can't be," another said back.

"It's me, Padalmo. Please listen to me. I am with-"

"I don't know who you are, but you are a terrible liar. My son is dead, and soon you shall be as well. The return of fire is at hand, darksider. You heathens will at last be stricken from the world."

"No father, it really is me. I am Padalmo Tala'Drog, son of Imalmo Tala'Drog. I was raised beside the waters of Drog'Chu. I have returned. I am with the seeders."

"Lies. Continue preparations. Do not lower the defenses."

"We are approaching the citadel," Moses said. A huge building stood up above the others. It was shaped like a tiered pyramid, shod with iron and without visible windows or openings.

Padalmo pleaded. "Don't you recognize my voice? Shall I name each one of your wives, from the first to last, and every mark they bear? Give me audience!"

"I can open a weak spot in the blast shield, if you like," Moses said to Padalmo. The prophet shook his head.

"I will be with you shortly, father," Padalmo said. "I will wait for you outside, with the seeders. Your faith shall compel you to listen."

*

The transport turned, presenting its long side of cool grey metal, but continued on its previous trajectory, sliding toward the open concrete platform in front of the pyramid-like citadel of Pana'Chu. The mechanized firing turrets that surrounded the citadel all shorted out with a burst of sparks and a grinding of gears. The long barrels of the cannons slowly slumped toward the ground, the men inside either screaming or dumbfounded by the sudden disabling of their weapons.

The transport slowly came to a rest of sorts in front of the citadel entrance, hovering a meter above the concrete slab. The wide doors to the temple-fortress slid open, and a troop of armored soldiers poured out, weapons at the ready. They opened fire, their automatic rifles barking, and the shield around the transport lit up in a bright orange as bullets deflected away. A few of them flew directly back, striking some

PROPHET OF THE GODSEED

of the soldiers. Blood splattered on the temple walls, but the firing continued.

The door of the ship slid open, and a gangplank extended itself down to the ground. Bullets continued to light up the shield as Padalmo, flanked by Anders and Moses, walked cautiously forward, pausing at the edge of the barrier. The company commander yelled loudly at the soldiers around him, and the firing died down. Wounded men were quickly attended to, but those that still stood kept their rifles trained on the trio.

Padalmo cleared his voice and said, as sternly as he could manage, "I am Padalmo Tala'Drog, son of Imalmo Tala'Drog. I have returned from the dead. You hold my own house against me. What say you?"

The company commander, still looking down his sights, shouted back. "We have been given orders to shoot on sight anyone claiming to be the son of the city lord."

"And so you have tried," Padalmo said. He breathed deeply in an attempt to calm his heart. "But I cannot be kept from rightful place of prophet, and we are now out of time. Let me pass or I will use force to overcome you."

"My orders stand," the commander said. "For the God Seed!"

Padalmo flinched and nearly fell backward as the commander charged, flanked by two other soldiers. He drew from his hip a sword that was painted black, curved and deadly, and dropped his rifle. The remaining men on the wings began to fire again, their bullets bouncing away from the shield. Padalmo felt a hand at his back steadying him, that of Anders, who he saw was wearing a faint smile.

Anders touched a button on his wristband, and the commander, along with every other soldier, toppled to the ground, screaming, their limbs twisted in agony and their backs curved stiffly. After another moment, the company seemed to give another collective shriek, and Padalmo could see blinding arcs of bright white lightning arcing between the men and the defense turrets.

"Don't worry, we haven't killed them," Moses said. Padalmo released his held breath. "It's a countermeasure that uses high voltage electricity to disable muscle control. They will recover in an hour or so."

Padalmo nodded as he felt Anders's hand pushing him forward. They passed through the transparent energy shield seamlessly, Padalmo feeling only a slight tingle of his skin as they did so, and approached the massive storm doors of the citadel. They stood iron-grey and eight meters high, and were shut closed. Padalmo reached forward and pounded on the door. Only silence answered them. He saw Anders and Moses remove their tablet devices from their belt loops.

"All this way, only to be shut out by the door," Padalmo said. "I should have thought of this."

"We are working on a solution," Moses said. "We've already cracked the internal network, but we are having trouble finding door control." The doors creaked, then slipped open a foot. Moses smiled. "There. I think Anders has got it figured out."

The door began to slowly slide open the rest of the way, revealing a long hallway with rows of bright incandescent lights above a floor bearing intricate artistic design. It appeared deserted.

"Anders says to lead the way," Moses said. "This is your house, after all."

Padalmo did his best to match Moses's calm and cheerful face, but found the weight in his chest to be too great to smile. His hands twitched with fear. With a deep breath, he walked into the citadel, the high temple of his family, his people, and his gods.

Their footsteps echoed as they walked the empty corridor. Soon it opened into a foyer, which in a normal situation would have been lit by dozens of skylights and light pipes that brought in the eternal sun, but now was lit dimly by pale emergency light fixtures. A mosaic covered the floor, depicting a stylized face overlooking dark shadowy human shapes. Huge paintings hung on the wall, only barely visible in the gloom.

One of these Padalmo recognized from his many visits before he left for the trial of the prophet. For a long while, it had been one of his favorites. It depicted the first prophet, Podastamu, walking through fire with a train of followers, their heads bent. In the dim light it appeared ghastly and unsettling, Podastamu's face looking mad with blank, open eyes. The flowers looked like shadows, walking in fear and torment. Padalmo turned away and walked toward another hallway.

"This will take us below, to the command center," he said. He heard Moses translating his words for Anders in the holy tongue. "The roots of the citadel are the oldest structures we have, dating all the way back to the last cleansing, some say even before, though it is blasphemy to say so. I've never been permitted to explore its true depths, but I hear that there are many chambers below, some as wide and encompassing as stadiums."

They found the stairs, which were marble clad and wide enough for ten men to walk abreast, and began descending. Their echoing footsteps grew with reverberation, and then became soft as they reached the bottom of the stairs. The decorated temple had turned into a fortress, with walls lined with steel and lit by fluorescent lights.

CHAPTER 9
Prophet

"Broadcast." Claribel stood behind her niece's workstation, watching her type furiously, her eyes darting between two large displays filled with code.

"I just need to test it, to see if the recipients truly overwrite their firmware after the virus is passed on," Tully said, her voice rising in pitch to a shrill cry.

"We're out of time. The live application will have to do. Send it out."

"We're not going to get a second chance at this. If they can adapt..." Tully looked back at the captain and shook her head. "Nevermind. I'm going to initiate the virus in the forward battalions. If they adapt, at least it will buy us some time."

Claribel nodded. Tully typed up a final section of code and let the computer compile the virus. After a few more keystrokes, she pushed her chair away from the console and put her hands behind her head.

"That's it, I'm finished. Nothing else to do."

Claribel looked at her tablet as her com chirped. "Not quite. Anders and Moses have gained access to the closed intranet of the defenders."

"Then what do they need me for?" Tully said.

"They don't necessarily need you, but I might. I want to make an attempt at eliminating control over their weapons detonations."

"Do you really think they are foolish enough to have anything besides a true manual control for launch or detonation?"

Claribel cracked a smile and seated herself at the station next to Tully. "Never assume intelligence or wisdom, especially with an unknown culture. Humanity is full of fools. We might have a few on our hands now." She brought up an interface showing a relay of the transport's computer, which in turn was operating automatic network cracking routines through the personal tablets and coms of Moses and Anders. "Besides, what else do we have to do?"

"How about sleep?" Tully said.

"Are you really going to be able to sleep through all of this?" Claribel said.

"Good point. At least I can get an audio stream going." Tully turned up the volume at her terminal, and heard Moses speaking in a strange language.

"Now you're hacking Anders's com, eh?"

"No, I'm tapping into Moses's hardware."

"Not any better."

"Fine, I'll turn it off," Tully said.

Claribel paused her frantic typing. "No. You should probably let them know we're listening though."

***

PROPHET OF THE GODSEED

"There's movement on the other side of that door," Moses said. He held up his tablet. "I can't make it out, but I think there are people on the other side."

Padalmo stopped in front of the heavy steel blast door. His ears picked up sounds, faintly, of a dull grind.

"This is the bastion of the citadel," he said quietly. Moses matched his tone as he translated into the Holy Tongue, which Padalmo realized that only now he was beginning to pick up. It was the rhythm; the steady long-short that all the scholars never knew about which confounded him. He sighed and refocused his mind. "Behind here will be my father Imalmo, and what is left of the elder cabal. We must convince them that we can end the threat of the Darksiders without them needing to unleash a new cleansing."

"Just a moment," Moses said. He spoke quickly with Anders, and then turned back. "We are going to erect another energy barrier, in case there are armed and hostile men on the other side of the door. Be aware that localizing the mass-energy field in such a way can only be done for a short time, and there may be severe spatial and chronological distortion."

"I don't know what that means," Padalmo said.

"Do not walk forward until I say," Moses said.

Padalmo nodded. He pounded on the door. There was no response. He raised an eyebrow at the sound of a female voice coming from Moses's location. Anders spoke to the voice quickly, and with an irritation that Padalmo needed no language to understand. Anders then set down a small case with a metal handle and pushed something on his tablet.

Padalmo gave a slight yelp as he felt a tremendous pressure exert itself on his eyes and eardrums. The door in front of him looked dim and wavering, and it felt as if it were pulling him in.

"This field is simulating extreme density," Moses said, gripping Padalmo's arm. "You may feel some attraction, though we are also suppressing a gravity well effect. It will lessen momentarily."

Padalmo watched as the field in front of him seemed to merge with the door, and the steel began to distort. It turned a bright, fire red, and then seemed to slowly collapse, ripped out of the wall. The burning steel hovered in the air, and then a faint glow from the room beyond crept into the cracks. As the field moved past, the door shredded into white-hot pieces that fell like charred rocks to the floor.

Padalmo could see figures on the other side of the field, looking distorted and motionless in a dimly lit room. The pressure lessened on Padalmo's ears. As his hearing returned, he could hear the crack of machine gun fire, both loud and muffled. The field lit up a bright orange in several places. It continued to move forward, and Padalmo found Moses pulling him forward a step at a time. Padalmo could hear shouts, though the humanoid figures beyond looked the same. He thought he could see the dark figures moving, but was uncertain, the blossoming orange in the mass field making vision difficult.

PROPHET OF THE GODSEED

"Stop! Stop!" Padalmo heard, though the field remained bright red. He saw shreds of metal- the remains of crushed bullets, falling toward the floor. The dropping continued for several more seconds.

The field went away, dropping more shreds of metal on the floor in a long arc just beyond the doorway. The figures visible in the shimmering mass field disappeared, and a brightly lit command room, with rows of computer terminals and large displays that was in many ways similar to the fire arc, came in to stark clarity. Men stood about the room, pistols and machine guns drawn; none of them stood where the visible humanoid figures in the mass field had stood.

Padalmo held in a scream. In a bloody heap on the floor, just past where the mass field had dissipated, lay the remains of what once had been a man. Clothes and body armor covered a mass of crushed bone and torn flesh without recognizable features. A twisted hunk of metal – probably a sword – was mixed into the lump, crushed by the gravity of the simulated mass shield.

"So it is you, Padalmo."

The prophet looked up at an aged man, white-haired and dark skinned with bright blue eyes. He was wearing body armor and held an automatic rifle casually. He looked to the score of men surrounding the door still, all middle-aged or older, the remnants of the war council and, he saw, the other Highlords.

"It is me, father," Padalmo said hoarsely.

"Cowardice I expected. Often it leads to betrayal, like the lovely Fala to me and then unto you. And cowards usually die hiding, as she did."

Padalmo's heart gave a shudder at his father's words. A part of his heart hurt at the thought, even though a bigger part thought it was a lie. As he stood there, with Moses to his side, he realized that his father spoke the truth, that Fala had betrayed him, and he also realized his foolish dream felt like just that; the reality of what he had seen muted all his desires. He swallowed hard and tried to harden his face.

Imalmo went on. "But now you have come forth to face me. Have I misjudged you?" Imalmo, the white haired man, waxed, almost to himself. "You must truly believe the lies of the Darksiders. It is a dark day for my family." With his eyes still fixed on his son, Imalmo shouted, "Let it begin!"

"No!" Padalmo shouted back. "I have come with the seeders. *I* am the prophet. Do you still not believe me?"

Imalmo looked away for a moment. "Forlano?"

"Preparing, sir. The initial detonation was a total success."

Imalmo looked back at his son. "What I have begun none can undo. Not even you, traitor. You are not the prophet. I am the prophet. It is *I* that does the will of the seeders. It is *I* that will remake the world in the image of righteousness."

"No, father," Padalmo said, his heart suddenly stuttering at his father's proclamation. He looked to the men that surrounded him. Each one wore a grim face, almost empty to Padalmo. He saw expression only on the face of his older brother Dimlo, who looked deathly afraid. "My father is not the prophet. You know that this is true. I stand with the seeders – these are two of them-" He looked back at Moses. "My friends."

"Lies," Imalmo said. "Heathens each."

"If they were truly the Seeders, they would have stopped the invasion of the heathens," an old man said from nearby. Padalmo recognized him from as many state visits – he was Fadasta, a Highlord.

"And we shall," Padalmo said. "Just as I shall stop you."

"Nothing can stop the firestorm now."

"You have already been stopped," Moses said.

"See? He even talks like a heathen," Imalmo said.

"Tully has successfully eliminated automated control," Moses said to Padalmo.

Imalmo cracked a smile that wrinkled his face. "I think these fools have shown all they have to bear." He raised his rifle. "Sorry, my son, but I cannot let you stand in the way of the rebirth." Men around him did the same.

With a reeling crash and a great, deafening hiss, the lights flickered and burst, or failing that, went instantly dark. The computer displays blinked out. Utter and total darkness fell on the room. Padalmo felt himself being pulled by the arm, back and away, as his ears were assaulted by a new cacophony. Muzzle flashes became the only light in the room. The high-pitched scream of ricochets echoed the blasts from the rifles. Padalmo felt burning debris from every direction.

Then, the shots ceased.

***

The citadel loomed at the end of the path. The defenders were scattering, defeated or dead. That is where the nuclear arsenal was held. Victory was at hand. The troop moved forward, pushed by an indomitable will and a constant stream of information. All the pushing forward, the constant flanking and re-attacks, the ever-straining loss of men and the need to kill; all of the effort had led to this last, final push. Troop carriers were dispatched to assist in the capture. At last, there would be peace on Terranostra.

Silence.

Sudden, alienating, horrible silence.

No data. No instructions. No way to tell what was happening on the battlefield and where.

No ability to call comrades, or friends. No way to call home to hear wife and child.

Alone.

Frandallo stood alone. He looked about him for his company comrades. He lowered his rifle. Where were they?

"Hello?" he rasped. He had not used his voice in... he realized he could not remember what it felt like to talk with his voice at all. "Where is everybody?" His voice hurt.

"Who is that?" A raspy voice said back. The rubble-filled street was empty.

PROPHET OF THE GODSEED

"Frandello."

"How do I know?"

"Can't you sense my uplink? Something's malfunctioned."

"I can't sense anything. I can't hear anything."

"Well I can't either," Frandello said back.

A man stepped out from behind a fractured, fallen wall. Combat goggles obscured his face. He pulled them down to his chin to reveal dark eyes set in pale flesh, the area of his face not previously covered now a stained grey from the grit of battle. Frandello did the same.

"I don't think I know you," the stranger said.

"Are you sure?" Frandello said. He stepped forward, his gun down.

"How can I be sure if I can't sense your uplink?"

Frandello shrugged. An old, strange gesture. "Do you know my face?"

"I guess. We probably need to get off the street and find the rest of the unit, see if we can get our uplinks repaired."

"Good idea," Frandello said. "Except..."

"Except what?"

Frandello ducked down and rushed to the rubble as he heard the sound of distant rifle fire. "Where was that from?"

"Can't tell. Here? No, it was quiet. Must be far away. What were you saying?"

Frandello nodded. "I don't remember why we came here, or even why I signed up for this."

"Me neither. Seemed like right thing to do, I suppose."

"What's your name?" Frandello said.

"Oh yeah, we can't sense uplinks. It's Balt."

"Strange place to die, isn't it?" Frandello said, peeking over the rubble.

"I never thought about it."

They both flinched as something rushed by overhead, almost too fast to be seen, kicking up dust and shattering windows below. Their ears hurt from the pressure as much as the sound.

"What the hell was that?" Balt said.

"Troop carrier?" Frandello said. "I don't know. Let's just get out of here, okay?"

"Right behind you."

*

The lights shuddered, blinking back to life in fits, bright and dim before their ballasts finally yielded steady, blue-tinted light on the battle room. Padalmo blinked, and realized he was on the ground, being held by Anders, who kneeled nearby, breathing heavily. The men in the room, the aged war council that had held command of the forces of Pana'Chu for many years, were scattered through the room. Many of them were on the floor, twitching like the troop of soldiers that had greeted Padalmo and the Seeders at the door to the citadel. Others were standing, looking dumbfounded. Weapons were scattered; some appeared broken, their bolts laying open or the receiver separated at odd angles. At the back of the room stood

PROPHET OF THE GODSEED

Vanessa, holding a metallic device that seemed to approximate a gun.

At the center of the room stood Malcolm Macbeth, his hands clasped behind his back in a relaxed stance. Even so, he appeared frightening and imposing. His pale blue eyes stared at Imalmo, unblinking, and his face betrayed no feeling of passion or fear. Moses, staggering up, spoke quickly to him. A voice, slightly mechanical in its rhythm, sounded from a device hanging at Malcolm's belt.

"The network is not responding, sir," it said, matching Moses's vocal tone and pitch, if not his true voice and rhythm. Moses's Darksider accent was replaced by one much more neutral. "I cannot function as your translator. I am sorry."

"No need to apologize," an echo of the patriarch's voice said. "Anders's translation matrix will do for now." Macbeth's eyes remained fixed on Imalmo.

"Who are you?" Imalmo said, wind rushing through the words as if he had been holding his breath.

"My name is Malcolm Macbeth. I seeded this world, and you are misusing my property."

Imalmo stared in disbelief. "It cannot be..."

"It is. Do not let your faith cause you to disbelieve." Macbeth turned and caught Padalmo's eye. "There was never any true Fire Ark. This was one, as was the place in the desert. Many holdouts designed to endure. Designed to house and protect the resources we needed to continue our journeys. The citadels in your cities, each, belong to us." He turned back to face Imalmo. "It speaks much to the spiritual and moral perversion of those who have the arrogance to call you your rulers. They destroy their people, their servants, their subjects, their families; all in the name of faith, but they themselves they hide away in shelters built by men with ten-thousand times their courage. Even when their prophet returns, they deny him, for that would reveal that they are true masters of nobody."

"You have no right to speak to me in such a way," Imalmo said, taking a step forward. He was checked by the raising of Vanessa's weapon.

"I have every right!" Malcolm said, his voice booming in the hollow room. "I have every right to judge you and to speak to you as I will. This is not because I am a god, but because I am a man. They are all men, here, and outside. I will speak as I will, and so shall they. Padalmo is your prophet. He shall lead, and you shall follow. We will take now what is rightfully ours. Impede us at your Peril."

"But, my lord," Imalmo croaked. "The Darksiders, the Adversary, they will-"

"We have ended your war. All of you! Step out into the sunlight, and burn away your illusions."

***

Padalmo looked out over the city of Pana'Chu. Pillars of black smoke erupted in many places, but the large buildings near the sea remained mostly intact, with some suffering superficial damage to glass and their external facades. Wind blew the hair of the

PROPHET OF THE GODSEED

prophet across his face. A storm was coming in from the Steaming Sea, softening the eternal sun. His brother Dimlo sat nearby with his head in his hands, refusing the sight.

"Rain, ever the purifier," he said, mostly to himself. "It washes away the dust of evil, and of perversion of good."

"You should write that down," Moses said through his electronic translator. He stood near at hand with Anders, who busied himself with his tablet as he leaned against the transport. "You are the prophet, after all."

"I am nothing," Padalmo said with a sigh.

"You should write that down too," Anders said. "I always liked proverbs that were short and sweet."

Padalmo found himself chuckling. "Me too. I always preferred simple sayings."

"Here's two that you should live by," Anders said. "Don't kill people. Don't take their stuff."

Padalmo nodded. "I shall try to live by it, and instill it in others, as you say." He turned as a few sets of footsteps sounded on the dust. Malcolm emerged from around a corner.

He smiled at Anders. "There's plenty in the vaults down below. Enough to power us for years to come."

"So you're glad we stopped by," Anders said.

"I am. Not a bad idea after all."

"Feeling like trusting my judgment?"

"Never. You have to convince me, as always."

"Of course." Anders looked over at Padalmo. "What are you going to do now?"

"I don't know. My first thought was to see if my father's house and harem still stand, but my brother has told me they were attacked by the Jaftans. My brothers and sisters are likely all dead."

"You could go make sure," Moses said. "We have transports. It would not take long."

"My first inclination is to take you up on that offer," Padalmo said. He looked down and shook his head. "Somebody should look into it, but not me."

"Why?" Moses asked.

"Fala, one of my Father's younger wives. I suppose we have unfinished business."

"What business?" Malcom said.

"It was she who convinced me to attempt the trial of the prophet, and it was she who conspired with me and Travole, my friend, to deceive all."

"You suspect betrayal?" Macbeth said. "Ever is it at work in the houses of the powerful."

Padalmo nodded. "I shall write that down. I do suspect betrayal, but of course, I was a betrayer, too, in my own fashion. It seems my father knew everything. Fala... I loved her, you know."

"Now seems like a good time to set that right," Anders said.

"No," Padalmo said. "That is from another life. I have returned a different person. Seeing things from your ship, my former concerns are petty. The betrayals are petty. Petty things must be beneath me, if I hope to forge a society that is worthy of the stars. Besides, my father's estate was one place of destruction among many, and I do not see how they have more value than all the others that are suffering now."

Macbeth nodded. "Had she not convinced you, petty betrayal or not, none of this would have happened," Macbeth said. "Keep that in mind when you see her, if you choose to see her. If you can see her."

"I will."

Malcolm looked out at the approaching storm. "I have tasks for you."

"Of course."

"I want you to broker peace. We'll be here only a short while to start it, so it must be you that finishes it. We have effectively disabled all of the network implants your enemies had. They will need help to regain the bits of humanity they have lost to collectivization. Your people must do this. You must work peacefully, and together." Malcolm reached in his pocket and handed a card to Padalmo.

"This is an important password. When your people have advanced enough to master simple space travel, you will find far above your world the quantum gate we assembled long ago. If you can reach it, and do the hardware repairs to restore its functionality, your society will have gained its right to rejoin the planetary network. That password will activate the gate."

Padalmo nodded. "It shall be done."

"What about your father?" Anders said. "The duty of his fate is yours as well."

"I suppose we must try him," Padalmo said. "He violated the law, and even a Highlord must never be above the law."

"Good words, prophet. Please excuse me," the chieftain said. "I have a lot of work to do." He walked away, back toward the citadel, as several more transports dropped out of the sky.

"You know, I've never felt rain," Moses said, looking at sun-obscuring storm rushing toward them.

Padalmo smiled. "Then let us take a walk." He looked down at the card Malcolm had given him, which had written in simple letters words he only vaguely understood:

Time fades away.

EPILOGUE
Black Coffee

Moses sat in front of the window, leaning back slightly in a padded chair beside a small table. He held in both hands a steaming mug. *Icarus* had, after rejoining its pieces, moved to a position above the habitable zone, giving the mess on Greywing a spectacular view of Terranostra. It hung in space like a banded marble, the side ever facing the sun a bleached white where clouds were not forming and rushing toward the dark, while the dark side looked like a pristine black dome of polished obsidian, though Moses knew that it was covered in white snow. In the middle was a belt of green where a billion people carried out lives that would be forever different.

Moses sipped the hot coffee and grimaced slightly.

"Not liking the brew today?" Moses turned to see Macbeth walking up, his own mug steaming. He stopped and stood beside Moses for a moment, staring at the planet below.

"It's Tully's favorite," Moses said. He looked into the dark brown liquid, nearly black. "I thought I would give it a try, since she's always drinking it."

"But you don't like it," Macbeth said. He walked around the table and pointed casually to the chair on the opposite side of the table. "May I?"

"Yes," Moses said. "I mean, no." He scratched his nose. "Yes, you may join me; no, I don't like the taste of the coffee. It's very bitter."

"You should try something a bit lighter to start," Macbeth said as he sat himself down. "Tully likes her coffee blacker than black."

"It looks like it's a few shades away from black," Moses said, looking in his cup.

Macbeth chuckled. "Just try adding cream and sugar until you like the taste."

"Then it would probably be too sweet," Moses said. "But I suppose I should take your advice."

"Your tastes are a lot like a child's," Macbeth said. "I don't mean that as an insult."

"I didn't take it as one."

"As you get older, you start needing more and more flavors to feel like you taste anything at all," Macbeth continued. He stood up, retrieved a small bowl of sugar from a nearby table, and put it beside Moses. "However, I've never known a child who didn't absolutely love sweets."

Moses put a few spoonfuls into his coffee and stirred. He took a quick sip. "Better. Much better, actually."

Macbeth smirked. "I happen to know that Tully doesn't actually take her coffee black. She loads it with sugar."

PROPHET OF THE GODSEED

"Then why did she tell me to make this type of coffee?"

"She's young. She wants to appear more mature, so she drinks an old man's coffee."

"How does a type coffee make one appear older?"

"It doesn't. Not to old men like me, anyway." Macbeth chuckled. "Maybe to her age peers. People are unique, but we all seem to follow the same patterns. When we are young, we long to be older. When we are old, we long to be younger. Longing and desire never ceases."

"I have nothing to compare," Moses said. "I don't long for anything."

Macbeth leaned over the table. "You sure about that? You're drinking something you knew you'd hate just because somebody else said they liked it."

Moses felt a sudden pang of embarrassment, and took a sip of coffee impulsively that burned his throat going down.

"I'm not blind, boy," Macbeth said, still smiling.

"Anders said that..." Moses coughed to clear his stinging throat.

"That what, I'd blow you out of the airlock?"

"Yes, actually."

Macbeth shrugged. "I'd like to say those days are behind me, but a man's passion for his blood seldom thins with age and wisdom. However, my temper is nothing compared to Tully's. I don't feel the least bit worried about her. You still should be, though."

Moses found himself smiling, and, he realized, blushing.

"Let's just change the subject, eh lad?" Malcolm said. He nodded toward the window. "Hell of a view, isn't it?

"It is." Moses cocked his head. "Is seeing like tasting? Will I need more and more to excite me visually?"

"The eye never has its fill of seeing, nor the ear its fill of hearing," Macbeth said. "That's from an ancient text, the book of Ecclesiastes, and it is as true today as it was all those ages ago. In many ways, sight is the opposite of taste. Your first reaction, as a child, is to accept the world around you as given, as the standard. Only different sights can be wondrous, or enjoyable. When you get old, that starts to change. You start to marvel at creation; you start to look at things you have seen countless time before and wonder at them. The universe is quite an awe-inspiring place, once you start to really look at it, and we are little more than apes, careening through the stars, far out of our depth."

"When Padalmo looked out the window, it was a... spiritual experience for him," Moses said. "But it was not so for me."

"Give it time."

"I won't see him again, will I?" Moses said.

"Not in this life," Macbeth said. "If we ever return here, he will have been centuries dead, but hopefully we will get to observe the legacy of his being in the shaping of his society."

"He was my friend. I shall miss him, I think."

"That is why we travel with family, Moses. When you sail the stars, time goes by without you. Those that are dear must be brought along, or else be lost to time. Time fades away, Moses, like a river running eternally past us."

"Why?" Moses said. "Why do we sail?"

"Because it is what we do. We are the seeders. It is also what we love. It is our purpose: building a humanity that spans the stars. I wouldn't trade it." Macbeth smiled and sipped his coffee.

Moses, contemplating what was said, sipped his own. He still didn't like it, but it did taste much better with sugar.

This concludes part one of Deep Time.
To get early access to the future books and a free gift from me, please join my mailing list at http://eepurl.com/cRtlqb or http://dvspress.com/list

BURDENS OF THE PATRIARCH

Deep Time is in actuality not an invention of my mind alone. The setting, characters, and scientific ideas were created with my screenwriting partner, Matthew J. Wellman as a joint product intended for television – a product which never came to fruition due to the practical realities of business back when we first envisioned Clan Macbeth travelling the stars. I didn't give up on the universe, malcontent to let Malcolm Macbeth languish in non-existence, and neither was Matt. What follows is part of his vision of *Deep Time,* a vision I think you will find at once familiar and unique. Enjoy it with a cup of black coffee for him.

**

"Everett-vi is the best candidate for the newest jump seed, Malcolm." Anders was saying but Malcolm Macbeth paid him no mind as he continued to watch over the engineers hard at work keeping the *Icarus's* engines at optimal performance. As always, since his rescue from Earth – the Human race's ancestral home, Moses remained at Macbeth's side as the silver-haired man always had something up his sleeve. Yes, it was always a lesson and though it irked him, Moses knew that if it hadn't been for Macbeth's clan rescuing him from orbit around the planet he would not only be dead, but oblivious to what that fate entailed.

"We've been at sixty-eight percent light speed for nearly a month, Malcolm. Any feud between you and Conner is well past turned to ash. It's been generations." Anders went on.

It was an ever mind bending shock to Moses to think that though he was just shy of middle aged in his thirty-eighth year, this entire crew had lived for hundreds of years. Well, hundreds of planet-side years. As they traveled closer to the speed of light, time slowed for them. It was seen to some as a curse; traveling into deep space to plant the quantum entangled particle that would allow human civilization to expand - to travel without the boundaries of relativity – to the outer reaches of the galaxy, only to return months later to find everyone you knew dead, but the great, great grandchildren dead as well.

"Conner had a small mind," Macbeth said after a time.

"Yes, and you've won," Anders said mockingly, "Can't you at least give his kin, *our* kin, a chance at something greater? A chance to expand Clan Macbeth into the furthest depths of deep space?"

Macbeth snorted. He was the image of composed confidence but not so long ago, he would smolder at the mere mention of Conner's name. Moses had been around the man long enough to see the iron grip Macbeth had over his composure; it showed no sign of slipping now.

PROPHET OF THE GODSEED

"We'll be in the Everett system in less than forty-five minutes," Anders said. "I would stop so that we at least consider the option given what cultural advances their sure to have developed."

"There'll be none, boy." Macbeth said. His tone wasn't mocking, it had a hint of... pity.

Anders heard only heard it though and the bitterness in his voice matched that of what he imagined was there in the older man. "He was the greatest engineer that had ever been aboard the *Icarus*, aboard the entire fleet maybe! Maybe he doesn't have thousands of lifetimes to complete his work, but surely he bore a strong seed in Everett-VI. The planet is sure to be ripe with innovation. You'll see. I'll hail you when we arrive." He turned then on the rough iron catwalk above the mass of engineers working on the engine below, boots clapping on the metallic surface as he made for the central lift to take him back to the bridge.

"Anders," Macbeth called.

The younger man stopped, turning his head over his shoulder. The barest recognition that the older man, the Patriarch of Clan Macbeth had addressed him.

"Stop at the outer ring. We'll see what they've done, lad, but I don't want to trigger a religious event if we decide to move on." Macbeth said.

Anders took a deep breath, nodded, then continued on toward the lift. He was gone a moment later. The two men were left alone on the catwalk with the thrum of the engine room.

"That seemed... cruel," Moses said.

Macbeth let out a deep sigh, still watching the men work below. "Cruel. Yes, I suppose it could be seen that way."

"You know that Conner was his best friend, right?"

Macbeth turned to him then his eyes were a deep emerald green. His severe gaze finally forced Moses to look away. It had been close to a year now – ship time – that Moses had been on board but still he was as a child to the rest of the crew. "What do you remember of your life before we found you, Moses?" he asked.

He paused at the odd change in topic, considering. "Images. Places mostly. The Omni-Core sent instructions directly into our implants," he said. He moved his hand instinctively to a round scar just behind his right eye. "I didn't really have much I needed to remember. I did what I had to do, and was told how to do it."

"So you've said before," Macbeth replied. "Did you ever have children?"

Children were always fuzzy to Moses. There were imprints of sharp images torn from his mind. "I believe so. I lived with a pair of children. We were attached in some way. I recall panic at the thought of harm coming to them. Could they have been mine?"

Macbeth let out a soft chuckle, "I suppose they could have been, at that. What would have hurt them back on Earth?"

The image tugged in Moses's mind. A white sheet with blue, yellow and brown on it. A drawing. A... bird. "Creativity," he said finally. "The Omni-Core strove for conformity." He had taken the drawing and hidden it away. Afraid someone would find it and take the little one away from him.

"And what would you say is the opposite of conformity, Moses?" Mac Beth said.

After a moment of thought he replied, "Autonomy. How you and your clan are showing me to live, Malcolm."

He turned on his boot heels and strode toward the central lift then. Moses turned to follow behind.

"An excellent answer, Moses. But are we showing you to be autonomous?"

"Well yes. If you recall, my first night aboard the *Icarus* I couldn't handle a broom," Moses said.

Macbeth stopped then, in front of the lift. "Yet you follow in my footsteps."

"Well, you instructed me to when we first—"

Macbeth faced him then, "Am I your new OmniCore, Moses?"

"I should hope not, Malcolm."

"Do you see where I'm going with this?"

"Not at all."

Macbeth turned and entered the lift as it opened before them. Moses hurried along after him. The two faced the doorway, Macbeth's steely composure quieting the small room as he stood at parade rest. Moses twitched nervously as the lift shifted into motion.

"We'll be approaching the Everett system in twenty ship minutes," a voice over the com announced.

"What does it mean to be human?" he asked.

Moses thought for a moment before answering, "To struggle."

A smile cracked on the lips of the Patriarch. "And why is it we struggle?"

"To understand. To know. To... be."

"All of these things, Moses, cannot exist if we were fully autonomous. Humanity needs itself to survive. It's why the clans came into existence in the first place," Macbeth said. "To be in deep space, we need family. With family, we struggle to find our place. Our usefulness."

"That often troubles me, Malcolm. If that's true, why have you kept me aboard?"

"That's a question for another time, Moses. Suffice it to say, your usefulness is constantly appealing to me." The doors opened and the two men continued down a long corridor. The rough metal paneling on the walls of the upper decks of the ship hadn't changed since the ship was originally constructed – according to some of the older crewmembers, Macbeth had a nostalgic streak and the aesthetics of the upper decks were a way of keeping him focused on his goal.

"To work together, to have community, we cannot be completely autonomous. There is a level of conformity among us. An agreement, shall we say, to work together toward the achievement of a greater goal." Macbeth said.

"So it is, in fact, conformity that you're showing me?" Moses asked.

"Don't be absurd," Macbeth replied. "If everyone knew how to manage the helm, and no one knew how to maintain the engines, how would we achieve anything? Our dream of deep-space travel would never have begun. No, Anders is a great helmsman and Timothy's ability to adapt our engines to the newest advances from our planet-side colonies is unmatched. In these things, our autonomy is priceless."

Moses considered this as the entered the bridge. The room spilled out from the door in a deep, downward sloping room. Descending the ramp, they passed console stations; navigation, communications, weapons. Their occupants busy at work. Anders was below at the helm.

"Status?" Macbeth asked.

"We've slowed to main thrusters. The anti-matter engines have disengaged," Anders said. "We'll be within scanner range shortly."

Moses followed Anders intense focus. He was obviously a skilled pilot. He'd taken the *Icarus* out of plenty of dangerous situations with little damage done to the ship. It was plain to see what Macbeth was talking about in Anders' ability. His skill was second to none in the Macbeth Clan.

"We should be within scanner range," Anders said.

"I'm picking up some serious tech, Patriarch," the tech behind them said, Macbeth rolled his eyes at the title. Moses still had problems with his short-term memory, so he hadn't gotten a grasp on everyone's name. He had begun to get the sense he should feel embarrassed, after all he had spent a year with these people.

Anders flashed a satisfied grin at Macbeth. "Whatever Conner's done, His people will be out colonizing half the quadrant for Clan Macbeth."

"Can you give us a visual, Vanessa?" Macbeth asked.

The woman nodded, dragging the image from her small monitor up to the grand viewing screen at the front of the room. The image of a gas giant sprung into view, blocking the light of a small yellow star. The *Icarus* slowly passed its horizon to reveal the small, terrestrial planet in the inner reaches of the solar system.

Anders gasped at the sight.

"All stop." Macbeth said.

Anders stared at the planet, not reacting to Macbeth's command.

"It's reached singularity, Anders. Stop the ship. Now."

Anders shook himself from the shock, first stopping their forward momentum then engaging the grav-anchor. He stood up, tears heavy in his eyes as he approached Macbeth. "You did this!" he shouted. "How bad was he that you could go so far as to annihilate an entire faction of our clan to settle your petty grudge?"

Macbeth stood still, his eyes never left the view screen.

Moses looked up at the planet. A swirl of satellites obscured the surface. He was grateful; somehow, he had avoided remembering the beauty of this planet. Somehow, he would be able to sleep tonight not knowing the full reason behind Anders' anger.

Anders brushed past Macbeth then, ignoring the cries of the rest of the crew. He needed time to grieve. In light of what was their most promising achievement this year, he needed his time to grieve.

"Jon," Macbeth said. "Can you take us out of the system on your own?"

"Sure thing, Macbeth." He said.

With that, Macbeth strode out of the room, back toward the upper deck corridor. Moses watched in silence.

Jon took the helm and guided them out of the solar system.

"Moses?"

He shook his head waking from his stupor. Jon was looking at him expectantly.

"He's not answering the com. Could you go find him?"

He looked around, seeing it was just the three of them on the bridge.

"Sure," he said and walked toward the corridor. He passed the woman again. *Vanessa .I'll remember this time.*

When he exited the bridge, Macbeth was nowhere in sight. Moses knew where he was, however.

Short term memory was a tricky thing. If he didn't repeat an action, a name, a place over and over again, he couldn't remember it. He knew Macbeth and his immediate family because of his consistent proximity to them. He knew Conner because frankly, he had been one of the few friends Moses had made outside of Macbeth's immediate family. He had been so wrapped up in the confusion of the planet, with the anger evident in Anders' face, he hadn't noticed the slow swelling of anger in his own chest.

He ran then, down the corridor, heedless of the protocols he was breaking. He veered right, past the observation crews pouring over scanning data. He turned again, and again heedless of the personnel he pushed out of the way. Finally, he stopped a lone door at the end of the maze.

The door to the nose of the ship opened and Macbeth stood at the tip of a catwalk surrounded by wide-open space on all sides. Moses took a hesitant step out. The vastness of space always made him motion sick so he stopped only a few paces in. "Why?" he asked.

"Are we automatons, Moses?" he asked, his back turned facing the depths of space.

"He was Anders' best friend! Your son's best friend, Macbeth! Why is Anders so upset? What happened to that planet?" Moses cried.

Macbeth turned then, his shoulders slumped. "The planet achieved singularity," he said. "Do you remember Earth when we found you?"

"You know I don't."

"But you remember the scars that occurred afterwards."

Moses turned away at that. He always felt a shiver of shame at his scars. None of the other clan-men had them; he wasn't even certain why he did.

"When a planet achieves singularity we must abandon it and all the people on it. An AI has taken a leadership role: delegating tasks, placing people best suited for each other together. Sound familiar?"

Moses nodded, "The Omni-Core."

"What happened to Earth happened to Everett-VI," Macbeth went on. "The 'Omni-Core' drafts any network capable device into its community and begins delegating tasks to it. If we got any closer, we would be put our entire fleet at risk." Macbeth turned back to the vast space before the nose of the ship.

Moses overcame the motion sickness and approached Macbeth on the catwalk. "Why did you leave Conner planet-side?" he asked.

"Hubris," he replied.

Moses stood shoulder to shoulder with him now, confusion writ in his eyes, "Hubris?"

"I am a prideful man, Moses. Anyone in this fleet can attest to that. When two prideful men stand toe-to-toe, people are liable to get hurt." Macbeth explained.

Moses was thoughtful for a moment. He realized, like Macbeth, he too was granted a sort of calm from gazing out into the vastness of the stars.

"So, Conner was too autonomous?" he asked. "And you needed him to conform, so that he could be part of the community."

Macbeth grunted. "You're learning." He said. "Life is ever a struggle for balance. We cannot be too dependent or too autonomous. In the end, we rely on each other to strike a balance and find our place."

"But Conner didn't find his place," Moses said. "You gave him an ultimatum."

"A choice, Moses. I gave him a choice. To follow the lead of his Patriarch, or see how we did on his own."

"So you knew if he was in charge, our best computer engineer, the entire civilization he built would fall into singularity?" Moses asked, aghast.

"There is always free will, Moses. It is the board on which we strive for balance."

"That doesn't seem like much of an answer for a man of such self-acclaimed hubris."

"Of course I knew, Moses!" He shouted. "He was my clan mate since he was born. Everyone in my crew has ties to me, and I them. If it hadn't been Everett-VI it would have been this entire damn fleet. Now you tell me, does arrogance negate self-preservation?"

Moses watched Macbeth as the fire twinkled in his eyes from burning rage down to glowing embers of regret. Macbeth turned back to the stars, hiding the weight on his heart.

"Was there no other option?" Moses asked.

"There was always another option. Conner had but chosen to make those decisions." With that, Macbeth fell silent.

The two stood out at the tip of the catwalk, watching the stars and the swirl of solar systems for a time.

"Free will is like a board," Moses said. "But you have to balance with everyone else around you."

"Aye," Macbeth said.

"And if you're not careful your weight can topple the board over, along with everyone on it."

Macbeth nodded and turned from the beauty of the cosmos to Moses, "Aye, lad. And in your innocence you find understanding; in your understanding I hope you can understand your worth to me."

With that, Macbeth turned from the stars and strode back onto into the bowels of the ship, leaving Moses to ponder the weight of that responsibility.

You can read more of Matt's work at http://matthewjwellman.com/

About the Author

David Van Dyke Stewart is an author, musician, YouTuber, and educator who currently lives in Modesto, California with his wife and son. He received his musical education as a student of legendary flamenco guitarist Juan Serrano and spent the majority of his 20s as a performer and teacher in California and Nevada before turning his attention to writing fiction, an even older passion than music. He is the author of *Muramasa: Blood Drinker, The Water of Awakening,* and the fairy tale *Garamesh and the Farmer* He is also the author of numerous novellas, essays, and short stories.

He can be found online at dvspress.com, davidvstewart.com, youtube.com/rpmfidel, and you can email him at stu@dvspress.com.

Sign up to his mailing list at dvspress.com/list for advance access to future projects and access to free books.

Printed in Great Britain
by Amazon